"Congratulations," Grant said. "You're a smart girl. You'll do well."

Laura let out a breathless laugh and turned down the path again. "So you're not one of those who think girls are good for nothing but marriage and motherhood?"

"Not when they're as smart as you are."

From the Wild Rose, the sound of the piano came faintly to Laura's ears. She could not remember when she had been so happy. She laughed again, dangerously close to tears.

"I'm so glad to hear you say that," she whispered.

"You're a remarkable girl, Laura MacKenzie," Grant said in a quiet voice.

He stood facing her, and Laura suddenly wanted him to take her in his arms. She felt dizzy and swayed on her feet with the force of emotion. Grant caught her.

"Laura, are you faint?" he asked.

"No, no," Laura whispered, closing her eyes and feeling the warmth of his hands against her skin. She knew she had never felt this before and knew that she was in love with him.

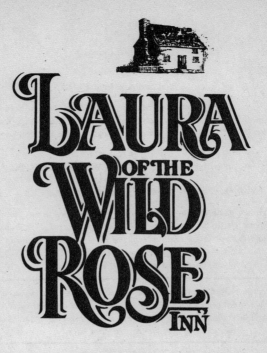

LAURA OF THE WILD ROSE INN

JENNIFER ARMSTRONG

BANTAM BOOKS
New York • Toronto • London • Sydney • Auckland

RL 5.0, age 012 and up

LAURA OF THE WILD ROSE INN

A Bantam Book/June 1994

The Starfire logo is a registered trademark of Bantam Books,
a division of Bantam Doubleday Dell Publishing Group, Inc.
Registered in U.S. Patent and Trademark Office and elsewhere.

ISBN 0-553-29910-7

Published simultaneously in the United States and Canada

Bantam Books are published by Bantam Books, a division of Bantam Doubleday
Dell Publishing Group, Inc. Its trademark, consisting of the words "Bantam
Books" and the portrayal of a rooster, is Registered in U.S. Patent and Trade-
mark Office and in other countries. Marca Registrada. Bantam Books, 1540
Broadway, New York, New York 10036.

PRINTED IN THE UNITED STATES OF AMERICA

OPM   0 9 8 7 6 5 4 3 2 1

LAURA OF THE WILD ROSE INN

1898

Chapter One

LAURA MACKENZIE BENT her head close as her friend Maggie Trelawney tapped her elbow.

"Do you see the cornet player?" Maggie whispered. "The second from the left? He's the handsomest fellow I've ever seen."

Laura smiled and glanced from side to side at the rows of respectable concertgoers.

"That's the *third* handsomest man you ever saw just today alone," she said, pitching her voice below the strains of the Vienna waltz.

"Maybe so, but I've decided once and for all." Maggie turned and made a face at Laura. "For the moment."

Laura stifled a laugh as she faced forward, and kept her attention on the band on the bluff overlooking Marblehead Harbor. From time to time, the bandleader looked back over his shoulder to smile and nod at the audience.

The park was filled with couples strolling arm in

1

arm, women in straw hats sitting on folding chairs, and children chasing their terriers through the crowds. With the Spanish-American War won in glory, all of Marblehead was in a mood to celebrate along with the summer yachtsmen who crowded the seaside town.

Laura relished the rare chance to relax and join the fun. She had a free evening when she could try not to worry about her parents and the Wild Rose Inn. For a moment, she closed her eyes and swayed in her seat in time to the romantic waltz tune.

"Can't you just picture the Vienna Woods?" she murmured to her friend. "The tall trees and the castles? Just like a romantic novel."

"I'm picturing the cornet player," Maggie whispered, twirling a miniature American flag between her fingers. She tucked the flag into her sash and sprang up. "Come on."

Before Laura knew what was happening, Maggie had taken her hand and was dragging her from their seats on the lawn. Laura grabbed the book she had brought along and hurried after her friend.

"Maggie, what are you doing? Oops! Beg your pardon, Mrs. Braxton," she called as she bumped into that lady's chair.

Maggie led the way to a cleared area on the grass. "I want to waltz. I can't sit still another moment. Let's dance," she said.

Laura swept back a loose curl of her blond hair and shook her head, stepping backward as two boys in

Rough Rider suits dodged between them. "You can't be serious."

"Oh, yes I am!"

The impetuous Maggie swept Laura into a waltz, and Laura could only laugh and follow along. Faster and faster the girls whirled around while the music filled the balmy August air. Laura grew dizzy with laughter and her book flew out of her hand, landing with a thump on the lawn.

Laughing and gasping, the girls broke apart as a young man stepped forward and stooped to retrieve the book.

"I think you dropped this, Miss," he said, standing up and holding it out to Laura. "Good evening."

Laura caught her breath and pressed one hand to her heated cheek. "Th-thank you," she stammered, taking the book from him.

"You're very welcome. Beautiful evening for a concert, isn't it?"

Laura was momentarily tongue-tied as she met his eyes. Maggie slipped her arm through Laura's and spoke for them both.

"We're having the most *delightful* time," Maggie caroled. "Aren't we, Laura MacKenzie?"

"Yes," Laura said, blushing at Maggie's none-too-subtle introduction.

"And everyone who had the privilege of seeing you dance is having a delightful time, too," he said with an admiring smile. Then he bowed, put on his straw boater, and walked away.

Maggie turned and gaped at Laura. "Did you see the way he looked at you?"

"He didn't look at me in any particular way," Laura said, tucking the book under her arm.

"He did too, and you know it," Maggie insisted, her green eyes sparkling. "You're blushing."

"I am not!"

"*And* you touched your hair when he turned away," Maggie added with a triumphant grin. "You're touching it again right now!"

Laura felt her cheeks flaming and she jerked her hand down from her hair. "I thought it was coming unpinned from dancing," she explained.

Maggie nodded sagely and then spluttered with laughter. "Oh, Laura, you silly goose."

"Goose, yourself, Maggie Trelawney." Laura spun on her heel and began to walk swiftly across the lawn, her white muslin dress whisking around her ankles.

Her friend's laughter followed her as Laura made her way through the park, and she quickly looked back and waved at Maggie to show that she was taking it in good spirit. Up ahead, she saw a familiar figure seated on a bench overlooking the harbor.

"Miss Shaw!"

Her former teacher turned, instantly smiling a welcome. "Laura, how nice to see you," she said as she patted the bench beside her. "How are your parents?"

"Well, thank you," Laura replied. "I thought you might be here. I've brought your book. Thank you so much for lending it to me."

4

Miss Shaw turned the volume over in her hands. "And how did you enjoy *Pride and Prejudice*?" she asked.

"Very much, thank you," Laura said. "I'd like to talk about it someday when I have time."

The older woman looked sharply at her. "I hope you don't have too much work at the inn? I'd hate to think you're not reading anymore."

Laura shook her head. As she looked out at the harbor she noticed the moored yachts in a crowd as thick as the throng of concertgoers in the park. She loved the Wild Rose Inn and Marblehead. Her home was a popular summer resort where the days and nights were busy. Not that the Wild Rose catered to wealthy tourists: far from it. But the yachting elite were buoyed up by a large population of seasonal, itinerant tradespeople and hangers-on. Since finishing her last year of school in June, Laura had been working at home full-time, and the moments were few that she could spend on herself. Her days and evenings were filled with chores, and most nights she was too tired to read. Miss Shaw's words interrupted her thoughts.

"You have a fine mind, Laura," Miss Shaw was saying in her schoolmistress tone. "I would very much regret seeing you drop all intellectual pursuits."

"I won't, Miss Shaw," Laura promised.

"And don't let your father use up every spare moment you have," her teacher continued with a prim shake of her head.

Laura smiled at Miss Shaw's strictness. She had spent ten years under the woman's tutelage and was always touched by how encouraging Miss Shaw was to her.

Her teacher turned *Pride and Prejudice* over in her hands again and brushed away a blade of grass. Miss Shaw's profile was stern, but there was dignity in her bearing and voice. She smiled up at Laura, her eyes suddenly warm.

"Are you enjoying the concert?"

Laura let out a happy sigh. "I adore it," she said. "What could be lovelier than this?" she added, spreading out her arms to encompass the view—the harbor with its bobbing, white-hulled boats; the jewel-toned sky; the blue-uniformed band; and the milling, murmurous crowd.

"I wish I could hold all of Marblehead in my arms for this one moment," Laura said. Then she blushed and glanced at her teacher. "I must sound very foolish."

"Not at all." Miss Shaw took one of Laura's hands in hers and pressed it warmly. "You have a wonderful capacity for enjoyment, Laura. Do not apologize for it."

Laura hid a self-conscious smile. "All right then, I won't."

"Enjoying life is a precious thing," Miss Shaw continued as she released Laura's hand, and sat looking out at the grand view. "In all the years I've lived in Marblehead, I've always taken the greatest pleasure from sitting here on this bench. I grew up in Salem, you know, and although it's only just around the corner, I never felt it had as pretty or inspiring a prospect as this one."

"I don't think there's a prettier view in all Massachusetts," Laura agreed. "There certainly is—"

She broke off, her words dying on her lips. The band had begun another tune. Laura had never heard music like this before. The melody was so tender, so achingly sweet, that after the space of three heartbeats, Laura felt a prickling of awe along her arms and back.

"Beautiful, isn't it?" Miss Shaw asked quietly. "It's from *La Bohème,* Puccini's newest opera."

"Oh, it's just heavenly," Laura said.

"Laura!"

With a start, Laura looked over her shoulder to see Maggie waving at her, the white sash around her waist a luminous banner in the twilight.

"There's Maggie," Laura said, with an apologetic glance at her teacher. "I should go."

"Maggie looks very pretty tonight, as usual," Miss Shaw observed. She turned her gaze on Laura and smiled. "Yet another new dress, if I'm not mistaken."

"Her brother Tink sends home his pay from the navy, and Maggie uses some of it to buy clothes," Laura said. She smoothed down the skirt of her own best dress, which was now three summers old. "Sometimes I think I'd like to be a lady of fashion, but I keep spending my money on books."

Miss Shaw laughed. "A more durable investment, I think."

Laura stood up. "Perhaps so. Thank you again for the book, Miss Shaw."

"Please come and visit me and we can discuss *Pride*

and Prejudice," the woman replied. "I will always be happy to see you at my door."

"I will, thank you."

Laura hurried away to rejoin her friend, who was beckoning urgently. The band finished its final offering, and the audience began to applaud and drift away over the springy turf. "What is it?" Laura asked. "You haven't already spotted the cornet-player's successor, have you?"

"No, silly, I simply can't stand around waiting for another moment," Maggie said in a melodramatic tone. "Come home with me, I want to show you what I've decided to order from the Sears, Roebuck catalog."

Laura chuckled. "What is it today?" she asked.

Her friend made a motion as though to pinch her, but Laura skipped away. "Well, maybe I do change my mind," Maggie said. "But the catalog is so chock-full of things to choose from."

"Ladies' fine millinery," Laura recited, striking a pose. "Hosiery of the best quality, guaranteed for life."

"Try our patent skin refresher!" Maggie said, striking a different pose.

"Try our hair tonic, try our liver pills, try our milking machines, try our trundle beds, try our bicycles!"

Maggie clasped her hands together with a reverent sigh. "The Sears, Roebuck catalog," she intoned. "Everything under the sun."

"And if you can't buy, at least you can look," Laura added. There was a trace of regret in her voice as she let her gaze drift over the departing crowds, hearing the soft whirring of bicycle wheels. Then she tucked her arm through Maggie's and smiled, and they set out down the road.

"Where do you suppose Jack was tonight?" Maggie asked. "He hardly ever leaves your side."

"I don't know. Jack Handy could be anywhere," Laura replied lightly. "It's of no concern to me."

"I say we drop in at the Ship and find out. It's on our way."

Laura stopped under a street lamp. "I thought you were so eager to show me what you want to order?"

"Changed my mind," Maggie said with an airy wave of her hand. "Come along."

Smiling, Laura followed Maggie's imperious command, and together they made their way to the Ship.

For two centuries, the Handys' Ship had been a rival establishment to the MacKenzies' Wild Rose Inn, and the two families had maintained a half-jesting, half-earnest antagonism down through the generations. Jack Handy, two years older than Laura and Maggie, had always gone against custom, however. From their childhood, Jack had carried a devotion to Laura as steadfast and unceasing as the wind. And although she had never returned his affection in the same way, she nevertheless counted him a loyal—if sometimes exasperating—friend.

The girls emerged from an alley, their shortcut bringing them out in front of the Ship tavern. Gas lamps blazed at the front door, where three local businessmen stood sipping their beer in the fresh air. The glow of the lamps was brilliant, sliding and glinting along the dewy sides of the beer mugs.

"I wish my parents would agree to put in gas," Laura said.

"Well, if it isn't Laura MacKenzie," joked one of the men at the door. He wiped his mouth with his sleeve. "Come over to join the enemy, have you?"

Maggie laughed. "Perhaps she's here to spy."

"Or perhaps I'm not even stopping in," Laura added.

A second-story window sash slid up, and Jack Handy poked his head out. "Laura! Maggie! Come on up!" he called. "You're just in time!"

"For what?" Maggie asked.

"I went to Boston today to pick up two packages," Jack answered.

"And what was in your packages?" Laura asked, tipping her head back to look at him.

He held up one finger. "First package: one cousin from New York, distantly related."

"New York isn't so distant," Laura teased.

"The society *he* lives in is," Jack shot back. He held up the next finger. "Second package: one porcelain bathtub from Sears, Roebuck, and I've just finished installing it."

"A bathtub?" Maggie echoed. Her eyes widened. "With *plumbing*? Let us see it, Jack!"

Jack looked at Laura when he spoke. "Aren't you surprised?"

Laura nodded slowly, and felt a strange, unsettling tug at her heart. The Ship now had a bathtub for its guests! Baths at the Wild Rose were efforts of heating water and lugging pails. Hardly realizing it, she took a step back.

"Come on up, it's the swellest thing!" Jack begged. "You won't regret it."

Maggie leaned close and whispered in Laura's ear. "You might as well. After all, this is your house anytime you say the word."

"I have a house," Laura said.

"I know. I know. I suppose a MacKenzie marrying a Handy is unthinkable!" Maggie murmured. "Still . . . Even if you don't want to see the bathtub, I'm dying to. Go on!"

Laura allowed herself to be shooed into the tavern, because even with the stab of envy, she was very eager to see the tub too. Both of them constantly marveled at the advances they saw springing up in the world around them. Inventions seemed to follow one another as swiftly as mackerel pouring from a net, and Laura sometimes found her imagination spinning in contemplation of a future that seemed just around the corner.

Their shoes clattered on the wooden steps as they hurried up the stairs. Jack appeared at the head of the staircase, a broad grin across his round, freckled face. His spiky red hair stood up from his head.

"You look as though you've been combing your hair with an eggbeater," Maggie said, giggling.

"Just wrestling with the tigers of progress," Jack boasted. "Ladies, may I present—the new bathtub!" He bowed and ushered them to a door on his right.

The girls both leaned in through the doorway and

gasped when they saw a gleaming porcelained iron tub whose claw feet clutched brass balls. Two polished taps and a curved spigot sat poised at the end of the tub like divers about to plunge in. A nearby oil lamp, still a standby in every house, glowed faintly on the brass fixtures.

"It's beautiful," Laura whispered.

"Extraordinary," Maggie marveled. "It is grand, isn't it?" Jack agreed, pushing past them and reaching for the taps. "Watch!"

Laura held her breath as he gave both handles a twist. Water gushed forth and splashed into the bottom of the tub. Stray drops caught the light like diamonds. Laura and Maggie stood watching the tub fill, and steam rose into their faces.

"No more lugging cans of hot water up the stairs," Jack said proudly. "No more slopping and sloshing! Get in, Laura, try it out!"

"I'm not getting in!" Laura retorted. "You've lost your mind."

"She's jealous, pay no attention," Maggie said.

"If you won't . . ." Jack climbed into the bathtub and sat down in the water, fully clothed.

"Jack!" Both girls rolled their eyes as he began pantomiming a bath, humming and splashing as happily as a duck.

"You're a fool, Jack Handy," Laura said with a laugh.

"A smart fool," he corrected her.

He lunged for Laura as though to drag her into the tub, but she quickly jumped out of his reach.

"Be careful!" Maggie cried as Laura bumped into the washstand, setting the oil lamp teetering.

Laura grabbed the lamp before it toppled and set it straight.

"That was close. Folks will say you're trying to burn down the competition," Maggie said.

"Don't be silly." Laura couldn't hide the nibble of resentment that was making her voice sharp, and she shook herself, as if to shake it off. She turned and made sure to give Jack a heartfelt smile. "The tub is wonderful. Thank you for showing it to us."

"Maybe your parents will put one in, too," Jack said encouragingly.

Laura shook her head and ran one finger along the gleaming faucet. It was warm to the touch. "I doubt it," she said. "They refuse to 'trick out our house with ridiculous new-fangled gadgets.' You know how my father feels about inventions."

An awkward silence descended. Mr. MacKenzie was known to be as stubborn as a barnacle and set in his ways about many things, and both of Laura's friends knew it well.

Maggie fiddled with her drawstring bag. "I guess your distant cousin is still distant," she said to Jack. "Unless you're hiding him in your pocket."

"He went off to the concert," Jack said, with his eyes anxiously on Laura.

Laura realized with a start that he and Maggie were trying to make conversation to cover her fit of melancholy. She extended her hand to Jack, and he took it.

13

"Congratulations," she said. "I'm sure your guests will heartily approve. And now, I expect our guests can use some attention from me."

"I have to go home, too," Maggie added, patting her dark hair as she looked in the mirror. "Good-bye, Jack."

Laura turned to leave the bathroom ahead of Maggie, wishing for the one-hundredth time that her parents would modernize the Wild Rose. Although charming and filled with history and memory, the old tavern was beginning to assume the air of a museum, and Laura wanted desperately to bring it into the future along with the rest of Marblehead. She herself felt ready to embrace the next century, and she wanted to take everyone and everything she loved into her arms with it.

Chapter Two

LAURA WALKED HOME in a thoughtful mood, and when she turned onto Front Street, she paused to consider the rambling house that loomed up above her.

The Wild Rose Inn had grown over the years just as the town—and the country—had grown. From its cramped beginnings, huddled on the edge of the continent between the wilderness and the sea, the Wild Rose had expanded over the years into a crazy quilt of additions, dormers, wings, and porches.

And yet, for all its size, the Wild Rose did have an antiquated look, as though it had been left over from another time. Laura thought it was like a grizzled mariner returned from years at sea, only to find his home changed beyond recognition in his absence. In the dark garden, crickets chirped and the scent of roses in bloom perfumed the air.

Shaking her head, Laura unlatched the garden gate and made her way to the kitchen door.

"Hello, Mother," she said as she went in. "Hello, boys."

Mrs. MacKenzie looked up from the dough she was kneading. The light from an oil lamp cast her and Laura's little brothers in a pool of yellow. "Ah, Laura, dear. How was the concert?"

"Very nice."

Laura poured herself a glass of root beer and walked to the kitchen table, where ten-year-old Henry and eight-year-old David sat drawing a map together in the lamplight.

"Treasure?" she asked, smoothing David's touseled hair as he bent over the work.

He hardly noticed. Henry was following his younger brother's progress with the watchful concentration of a hawk. "Remember, don't draw the *X*," he warned.

"I won't," David muttered.

Laura smiled and sat down across from their mother. She watched for a moment as Mrs. MacKenzie worked, and then gazed down into her glass.

"The Ship has just installed a bathtub, Mother. I've just come from seeing it."

"Oh?" Mrs. MacKenzie did not look up from her kneading.

Laura leaned forward. "Yes, and it's so elegant. Imagine not having to carry water back and forth."

"Trust the Handys to throw their money away on

16

these crazy contrivances," Mrs. MacKenzie grumbled. She wiped her hands on her apron, looking down at Laura with a complacent smile. "They'll look mighty foolish when it breaks for the first time, I've no doubt."

The MacKenzies' own indoor pump had frozen up three winters earlier, and was now unusable, so all the inn's water had to come from the well-pump in the yard. Laura glanced at the useless fixture at the dry sink in the corner and frowned down into her glass. The boys whispered to one another, pointing with ink-stained fingers at features of their map, all their attention fixed on their project. Laura watched them for a moment and then drew a deep breath.

"I think the Handys are smart to want to move ahead with the times," she told Mrs. MacKenzie, deliberately reviving an old argument. "They haven't had any trouble at all with the gas, and it makes a wonderful light. Everyone in town who has gaslight loves it. We're one of the few houses that isn't changing."

"These old lamps have always been good enough for us," her mother insisted. "Nor have we ever suffered by comparison to the Handys either."

Impatiently, Laura stood up and paced the old-fashioned kitchen, twitching aside the gingham curtains at the window and gazing at her own reflection against the darkness. "Sometimes I think you and Father insist on not modernizing simply because the Handys have," she mumbled.

"What was that, dear?" Mrs. MacKenzie asked.

"Nothing," Laura said. "But can't we lay aside this

17

old feud between us and the Ship? It's all ancient history, now."

Mrs. MacKenzie looked searchingly into her eyes. "Then it is true what they say."

Laura frowned. "What is?"

"About you and Jack," her mother replied in a tone of dismay. She looked truly stricken.

"Oh, Mother." Laura resumed her restless pacing. "I wouldn't be at all surprised if any rumor about me and Jack got its start with him and his wishful thinking."

"Wishful thinking, I should say so," her mother said, sinking into a chair. "They will never cease trying to get the upper hand of the MacKenzies. They won't stop until they get the Rose."

Henry looked up at that, a serious frown on his face. "I'll get the Rose, won't I, Ma?"

"You will, dear," Mrs. MacKenzie assured him. She looked meaningfully at Laura, who stood by the window again. "As long as Jack Handy minds his own business."

Laura bristled with indignation. "Isn't it possible he'd care for me no matter what my last name is, or where I live?" she said, hotly. "You know Jack doesn't have a calculating bone in his body."

"I know no such thing," her mother said stubbornly. "All I do know is that if the Handys have tubs and gaslights and—and—" She waved both hands, as though shooing away a swarm of gnats. "If they've got it, *we* don't need it."

"But this has nothing to do with the Handys!" Laura turned around and crossed quickly to her mother, kneel-

18

ing before her. "Nineteen hundred is just around the corner, but we're stuck, stuck in the past. Everything's changing except for us. Maggie's going out to that new hotel on the Neck when they start hiring, and I don't blame her wanting to be in such an up-and-coming position."

The oil lamp flared up briefly on the table beside them, and then subsided again into its soft glow.

"Where Maggie Trelawney works or doesn't work makes no difference to the running of our hotel," Mrs. MacKenzie said. "I haven't had any complaints about the Rose."

Laura suppressed an impatient retort.

"And besides," Mrs. MacKenzie continued, wiping her hands on her apron. "After what your father went through as a child, don't expect you can ever change his mind about new techniques or machines."

"I know, Mother." Laura sighed over an old heartache. "I know Grandfather nearly lost everything on that patent steel-manufacturing process after the war, but this is different."

"Different or not, we don't have . . ." Mrs. MacKenzie looked at the boys, who were busy with their map again, and lowered her voice. "We don't have the money to fritter away on gadgetry. If you don't know that already then you should. Worrying about money is all your father does, and I'm afraid it's wearing on his health. Now go on into the tavern, Laura. Your father can use some help."

With a sigh, Laura stood up and reached for an

apron to tie around her waist. She knew perfectly well that business was not good, and except for an Irish girl who came on wash days, they had no help. Between Mr. and Mrs. MacKenzie, and Laura and her two small brothers, the Wild Rose Inn was barely clinging to its perch on Marblehead's rocky shore.

Laura walked through the dark corridor to the tavern, and paused at the door. She could remember earlier times when the place had been livelier, when loud laughter and cheerful voices had rung out from every corner of the inn.

But as more and more places in town had modernized, and the Wild Rose had stayed as it was, the younger patrons had sought out other watering holes, leaving behind the men who still thought of the telegraph as a startling innovation. For her parents' sake, but mostly for her brothers', she wished she could revive the business and lift it up into the next century.

"Laura?"

The door swung outward, almost knocking into her. Mr. MacKenzie was silhouetted against the light from the tavern.

"I'm here, Father," Laura said.

"Ah, good. Come in, come in." Mr. MacKenzie beckoned her forward, and Laura stepped into the oldest part of the Wild Rose.

Darkened beams stretched across the ceiling, and a massive fireplace with an iron crane inside it occupied one end of the room. At the tables and bar, a crowd of men enjoyed their evening beer by the light of the oil lamps. Laura felt an aching tug at her heart as she gazed upon the familiar faces.

"Hello, Laura," said a voice at her elbow.

Turning, Laura saw Mr. Carter, her classmate Louisa's widowed father, the editor and sole proprietor of a small weekly newspaper. He was sitting at a table in the corner, eating a bowl of oyster soup and reading a Boston paper. His unruly hair curled over his shirt collar, with only a few traces of gray among the black, and he smiled at her warmly.

"Hello, Mr. Carter," she said. "Taking a break from work?"

He wiped his hands on a napkin. "My Linotype machine is acting up again. I thought I should get away for a few moments, or else I might have thrown the whole contraption into the harbor and let the fish tangle with it."

A shrunken, bald-headed, side-whiskered man sitting nearby chuckled. "I remember when printers set their type by hand," he announced with satisfaction. "One letter at a time. B'God, they had to mind their *p*'s and *q*'s, I'll tell you. They didn't have these newfangled contraptions always breaking down *then,* did they?"

Two other men laughed approvingly, and Laura and Mr. Carter exchanged the long-suffering smiles of allies.

"No, Mr. Ledue, they didn't," Mr. Carter agreed patiently. "But even the best of them couldn't set type as fast or as accurately as a good Linotype machine can."

"When it's working," interjected another man, digging his neighbor in the ribs.

21

There was another round of laughter, and Mr. Ledue leaned toward Mr. Carter, one bony finger outstretched. "Speed is no great virtue, sir. I counsel you to remember that."

"I will," Mr. Carter agreed with a diplomatic smile.

Laura picked up his empty soup bowl as the other men fell back into their conversation. "Do you suppose they'd object to the invention of the wheel, if that were a new thing today?" she asked Mr. Carter.

The editor laughed heartily. "I wouldn't be at all surprised if some of the old sailors in here would. I believe some of them have *never* been in a conveyance that didn't float."

"I enjoyed your editorial about the automobile," Laura told him. "Do you really suppose they'll become commonplace?"

"I do," Mr. Carter said. "Why, just the other day I was out at that grand spanking new hotel to get a quote from the owner, and he drove up in a grand spanking new automobile."

"Laura?" Mr. MacKenzie stood behind the bar, holding up two glasses of beer. He nodded toward a pair of men sitting at another table.

"Excuse me," Laura said to Mr. Carter.

As she made her way across the room, snatches of conversation washed around Laura like the tiny waves on a twilit beach. Many of the old-timers hoisted the same flag every night, reminiscing about the glory days of Marblehead's now-diminished fishing fleet, grumbling over the rich summer folk who cluttered up the coast with their fancy yachts. In their eyes, Laura imagined she saw a hint of baffled sadness, as though they couldn't quite believe they had gotten so old, and that things had changed so much since their youth.

"I didn't see you at the concert this evening, Mr. Penworthy," she said to an old fellow as she set his drink before him.

"Ah, no, no you didn't," he agreed. He fingered his unfashionable full beard and shook his head. "I can't say I care for this modern music, myself."

"Yankee Doodle Dandy isn't exactly modern," Laura teased.

"Ah, did they play that?" he asked, brightening at thoughts of his Union Army days. "I do love the old songs. 'When Johnny Comes Marching Home'—now there's a first-rate tune for you."

"They wouldn't play that," broke in Mr. MacKenzie. "Those concerts cater to the summer people, we all know that. And they want to hear that high-society music, such as I have no doubt they'll play all the night long at that jumped-up new hotel out there on the Neck."

There was a general grouch and grumble among the men. Laura shook her head with a mixture of fondness and frustration, and then turned as someone tapped her shoulder.

"Play us some songs, Laura," piped Mr. Ledue.

"Gladly." She seated herself at the upright piano and shuffled through the piles of dog-eared sheet music. "What will we have?"

" 'Lorena,' " suggested one man.

23

" 'Sweet Betsey From Pike,' " offered another as the men crowded around.

Laura brought her hands up to the keys, but left them poised just above. The songs they wanted to hear were all old songs, songs first in fashion during the Civil War. For a moment, she felt herself hemmed in, surrounded by the past. The old men, the old conversations, the old habits and ways—she was tied to them there at the Wild Rose, and she felt an instant of panic at the thought that this was to be her future. She glanced up at Mr. Ledue's kindly, wrinkled face, and he nodded at her encouragingly.

"Go on, Laura, give us a song," he said.

"Perhaps she has other plans than to sit and entertain a parcel of old dry-bones like us," came Mr. Carter's voice.

Laura laughed, and her alarm dissolved as quickly as it had arisen. "No, I don't mind, really."

Mr. Ledue grinned at her. "I expect we do seem a bit dusty to you, eh, young lady? Don't worry, you'll soon be married and will have the conversations of little ones to enjoy."

"Perhaps I won't marry right away," Laura said, bending her head over the keys and carefully picking out a melody.

There was some indulgent laughter around her. "Don't tell us you're one of those independent females," Mr. Trelawney hooted. "Thinking women should vote and suchlike."

"Wouldn't you trust your own daughter with a vote?" Laura asked him.

"Maggie?" Mr. Trelawney tucked his chin into his throat. "She wouldn't want it if I gave it to her," he said confidently.

"Well, I've never known Maggie to be without an opinion," Laura replied.

"My wife, God rest her soul, surely never let an opinion go once she laid hold of it, that's certain," Mr. Penworthy said. "She was a corker."

A bottle-maker named Crickle set his empty glass down on the piano with a thump, and all eyes turned to him. "Those women, like that Susan B. Anthony—in my opinion she is an unnatural woman."

"Hear, hear," muttered someone in the back of the crowd.

"She's now president of the National Woman Suffrage Association," Mr. Carter said into the silence.

"Exactly my point!" Mr. Crickle said. "Unnatural! Abandoning her God-appointed role as wife and mother. A woman may lead by example of her virtue and sweet temper, not by such a manly grasping for power and influence."

"I do agree with you," Mr. Trelawney rumbled.

Laura stood up abruptly from the piano. She placed one hand to her cheek, trying to catch her breath.

"Feeling vaporish, Laura?" asked her father.

"My apron is too tight," she said, struggling to untie it. She fought another rising wave of panic. The men

25

watched her in puzzled silence, as at last, she yanked the apron off.

"Oh, there," she said, breathing again. With a sigh of relief, Laura stepped away from the piano, and the men parted to let her through.

"I'm sorry," she said, suddenly embarrassed to have made such a spectacle of herself. "I think I'm a little tired —the concert—and—excuse me."

With her last words of apology, she picked up a lamp and hurried out, fumbling with the worn iron thumb latch on the door at the back of the room. Hitching her skirts in one hand, she hurried up the narrow staircase, the lamplight flowing up the walls around her.

In her room under the eaves of the old building, she sank into a chair at the open window and rested her elbows on the sill. For a few moments, she looked out into the night, letting her thoughts drift on the distant murmur of the ocean. Then she took her journal from the table by the bedside and opened it to the first fresh page, absently waving away a mosquito.

"Evening concert in celebration of our victory over the Spanish in Cuba," she wrote. "Overheard two men discuss lecture at National Geographic Society on Sven Hedin's explorations in Tibet."

Laura slowly lowered her fountain pen and gazed at the lamp, her eyes filled with visions of faraway places. When she looked back at her journal, the page seemed dimmer and harder to read than before, as though her eyes had been dazzled by the sun on distant mountainsides, or by the stars in the desert.

With a preoccupied frown, she pulled the old lamp nearer to her page. "I want to be a part of what is coming," she wrote. "I want to be at the front of the crowd so I can see it all."

She underlined the last sentence, the hard stroke of her pen like a whispered *yes* in the quiet room.

Chapter Three

"It's too hot for more than one person in here," Mrs. MacKenzie said, mopping her forehead with a flour-sack towel the next day. She slammed the oven door on a pair of peach pies. "Go on outside somewhere, Laura."

For a moment, Laura stood at the window and fanned herself with the hem of her apron. She gazed out at the town and stretched with a lazy, summer-afternoon yawn. Down the street, she saw Miss Shaw speaking to Mrs. Braxton, and then turn the corner and disappear.

"I saw Miss Shaw last night at the concert," Laura mentioned. "She's a remarkable person, don't you think? So strict, but so kind to me, always. And she talks about interesting things."

Mrs. MacKenzie shrugged. "Julia Shaw never did run out of conversation when I knew her, and showed no signs that she ever would," she said.

"Did you know her when you were both girls,

Mother?" Laura asked. She leaned against the window-sill, letting the breeze cool her neck. "She's from Salem, she told me."

"Yes," her mother said. "I knew her and so did your father. But that was a long time ago. Now I thought I told you to scoot from my kitchen. When I want to discuss schoolteachers, I'll go to school. Now, off with you!"

Smiling, Laura plucked her hat from a hook, kissed her mother's red cheek, and let herself out the back door. In the garden, she paused to break off some sprigs of lavender and then, weaving the stems into the blond hair piled up on the back of her head, Laura ambled down the street. She had a pleasant feeling of aimless-ness.

In the commercial center of town, Laura walked slowly, gazing at the gaudy come-hither displays in shop windows. One dress shop boasted the newest Paris fash-ions; a gents' shop bragged it carried celluloid shirt col-lars for every size neck; and Mrs. Delahay's Crystal Emporium beckoned the passerby to admire the finest finger bowls, celery boats, and sardine dishes. Laura was amused to note the sign in Mrs. Delahay's window that offered to teach housewives how to fold napkins "à la the Prince of Wales's Feather."

On a nearby corner, a ragman had set up his cart full of odds and ends, and Laura stopped to look through an old stereoscopic viewer.

"I can throw in some nice views of the Yosemite Valley out in California with that," the tinker said, squinting at her as though judging her pocket money by the look of her face.

Laura nodded, and then caught a glimpse of Jack Handy coming around the corner. A cowardly impulse to hide from his steady attentions made her turn around quickly, pull her hat brim down, and hold the viewer up to her face again. As she feigned concentration on the photographs, she heard his familiar voice behind her on the sidewalk.

"I'll turn you loose until dinnertime, Grant," he said heartily. "I'm sorry I can't show you around town, but I guess you'll make out fine on your own."

Laura lowered the stereoscope a fraction, and peeked over her shoulder just in time to see Jack clap a young man on the shoulder and then walk away. She recognized Jack's companion: he had retrieved her book for her at the concert. The memory of his smile made the color rush into Laura's face so unexpectedly that when he began to walk her way, she quickly put the peddler's wares back on the cart.

"Not today," she said, hurrying along. She slipped into Mr. Hammond's book shop, not stopping to question why she had been in such a fever to avoid Jack's friend.

The bell over the door jingled as she burst in, and Mr. Hammond looked up over the tops of his smudged spectacles at her.

"Laura MacKenzie, how do you do?" he shouted at her. He always spoke in the loudest and most urgent tones, as though hailing a lifeboat from the deck of a sinking ship.

Laura tried not to flinch at his voice. "Very well, Mr. Hammond," she replied, glancing furtively out the window. "Umm . . . do you have any new one-cent song sheets?"

"A heap of 'em!" Mr. Hammond bellowed. He led the way through shelves of books to the back of the shop. "Just came in the other day. Some real catchy tunes too."

Suddenly Laura snapped her fingers. "I've just remembered a lovely tune I heard last night. Do you happen to have a piano score for *La Bohème*?"

Mr. Hammond stopped and looked back at her in surprise. "Well, if that don't beat everything! I got that in the other day. I never thought it would sell!" He began searching among boxes and cartons. "Got to be here somewhere! Saw it just this morning. *Aha!*"

The doorbell tinkled at the front of the shop as another customer entered. "Here you are, Laura!" Mr. Hammond said.

"Thank you," she replied, glad for the score, and even gladder at the prospect of being left in peace. "Don't let me keep you. I'll just look this over."

"Take all the time you need." Mr. Hammond bustled past her.

From the front of the shop, a low murmuring voice asked something of the bookseller, and Mr. Hammond cheerfully replied. Laura opened the opera music, curious to learn the story that went with the beautiful melody.

But to her disappointment, the libretto was in Italian.

"Oh, dear," she sighed, as she riffled the pages. "I should have known."

Up front, the bookseller was shouting away, and Laura sneaked a look to see how his latest customer was faring under the vocal barrage.

It was Jack's companion. Laura quickly ducked out of sight behind a stack of leather-bound Shakespeares, but then peeked around the corner again, her heart hammering. The young man was talking amiably to Mr. Hammond, enduring the shopkeeper's deafening conversation with good grace.

From her vantage point, Laura made a study of him. His hair was as blond as hers was, but not curly; it was combed smoothly back from his forehead. His handsome face was lean and angular, his nose patrician. She had seen enough wealthy tourists to realize that his clothes were quite expensive, and his shoes were polished to a fare-thee-well shine: he was no doubt one of the Ship's fashionable patrons.

Laura found herself wishing yet again that her family would modernize the Wild Rose, in order to attract just such patrons. Before she could catch herself, she had stamped her heel in a gesture of frustration, and a precarious tower of books toppled to the floor beside her.

"Laura MacKenzie!" Mr. Hammond yelled.

Laura let out a squeak of surprise and embarrassment, and the young man turned and met her eyes for one horrifying, humiliating moment. Laura felt her cheeks flood with heat to be caught spying.

She gulped and began picking up volumes. "I'm sorry, Mr. Hammond. I'll set it right!"

"Oh, never mind that, Laura. Those opera songs are in Italian, did I mention it?" the proprietor boomed from the front of the shop.

"I see that, Mr. Hammond," Laura replied, wishing she might disappear.

To her further embarrassment, the young man began to walk toward her where she knelt among the scattered books.

"Are you an opera lover?" he asked, holding out his hand for the score. "I'd be happy to translate if your Italian is rusty."

"I don't have any Italian at all to go rusty," Laura replied, handing up the music with a feeling of resignation. She stood reluctantly, brushing off her skirt.

He turned the music to examine the cover, and instantly gave Laura a breathtaking smile. *"La Bohème!* I saw it last year in London. It was superb! Do you know it?"

"N-no—I only heard one of the tunes at a concert," Laura stammered, not wanting to admit that she recognized him from the night before. It would seem so brazen, so unladylike, especially coming on top of her espionage.

"Last night," he said, still smiling at her. "Did you enjoy the program?"

33

It was no use pretending anymore that she didn't remember their encounter. She let her breath out in a laugh. "It was very nice," she said. "And thank you again for rescuing my book."

"It was my pleasure," he said.

Laura found herself gazing up at him with an idiotic smile on her face. Blushing again, she looked down at the music. "Do you know the song they played from this?" she asked in some confusion.

"Yes, it was 'Che gelida manina,'" he replied, flipping through the score. "The setting is Paris, and a pair of Bohemians, a poet and a painter, are shivering in their attic apartment. Marcello the painter goes out to a café, leaving Rodolfo alone in the garret. Then, there's a knock at the door, and in comes Mimi, the pretty seamstress from downstairs." He broke off in a dramatic pause.

"And?" Laura pressed eagerly.

He smiled and handed her the score. His eyes were Delft blue. "Her candle has gone out, and he offers to light it for her, but first, he takes her hand in the dark and says it is so cold—that is what this song is about. They fall in love, and the curtain falls on Act I."

"Just like that?" Laura asked, arching her eyebrows.

With a laugh, he agreed, "Just like that. I suppose Bohemians are less inhibited than most about falling in love. They don't waste time taking walks and having tea."

"No, they're too busy creating beautiful music and paintings and poems," Laura said, her voice wistful.

"The things most worth doing," he agreed. "They defy convention in order to pursue truth and beauty."

Laura looked at him with fresh curiosity. "You've been to London, you said. Have you seen Paris? I'm sure it must be the most wonderful place in the world."

He nodded. "It is," he replied simply. "You would love it."

"Oh." Laura sighed and clasped the music to her heart. She was pleased to have met someone with taste and education, someone who spoke to her about the outside world.

"Are you staying at the Ship?" she brought out at last. "I—I noticed you speaking to Jack Handy."

"I am staying there. I'm Jack's cousin, Grant Van Doren." Grant held out his hand. "I'm visiting for a few weeks before going back to Yale."

"*You're* the cousin?" she asked as she shook his hand. She felt as surprised as if he had just sprouted wings.

Grant laughed. "What were you expecting?"

"Oh, well, I . . ." Laura bit her lip and gave him a rueful smile. "I guess that wasn't very gracious of me, was it?"

"It would help to know if I surpass expectation or fall short of it," Grant said.

Laura made a vague, self-conscious gesture with one hand, not quite knowing how to answer. "It's only that I never knew Jack had a cousin at Yale. In fact, I never knew Jack had a cousin from New York at all until yesterday," she admitted.

"Maybe he's ashamed of me," Grant said wryly.

She laughed. "I doubt that."

They stood grinning like conspirators for a moment. Then Laura reluctantly broke away. "I should be getting home," she said, walking toward the front of the shop.

Grant fell into step beside her. "Are you going to take the Puccini?"

"Yes. If I can stand close enough to Mr. Hammond without having my ears shouted off," she whispered.

Laura stepped up to the bookseller's desk. "Could you put this on my account, Mr. Hammond?" she asked. "I'd very much like to take it."

"That's grand, Laura, just grand!" Mr. Hammond beamed at her as he wrapped the book up in brown paper. "Glad to know you spend your pennies here when you get 'em, and not at the hat shop!"

"No, I suppose I'm stuck with this old hat," Laura said. Grant carried the parcel for her, and they walked out of the shop onto the sidewalk.

"Most girls *would* rather spend their money on hats than books," Grant said as he fell into step beside her.

Laura smiled thoughtfully. "Many, perhaps. I don't know if it's most. But at any rate," she added, "where I'm concerned, it's such a small amount of money it hardly tilts the scales at all. Most of the time I have to be satisfied taking books from the circulating library. But I do—" She broke off and shook her head.

"But you what?" Grant asked.

"I love to sit in my chair and look at a row of books

36

and know they're mine," she admitted, looking up at him in some embarrassment.

"And know that you can read them whenever you want?" he said.

"Yes. It must be wonderful for you to be at Yale, where you are expected to do nothing but sit and read."

Grant looked at her in surprise. "You make it sound about on par with getting into heaven."

"Well, I hope I can find time to read before I get *there*," Laura replied.

Their way led them through the narrow alleys and side streets of the town, and Laura turned toward the harbor as they continued to speak. The sun blazed down, and a salty bite was in the air. As she followed the flight of a gull with her eyes, Laura felt a wonderful sense of freedom. Still talking, they stood on a dock to watch the comings and goings of boats. The crews of yacht and fishing boat alike scrambled about their vessels on their tasks, coiling brown, bristling ropes, checking fittings and instruments.

"It won't be long before boats can sail themselves," Grant said. "And the crews will be obsolete."

Laura quirked one eyebrow. "I doubt that. If you live by the ocean you learn that men are more to a boat than machines to make it sail."

"But that's my whole point." He looked at her seriously. "Technology is moving forward, and the astute man will move with it. If man is more than a machine, why should he perform the tasks of a machine? Why be burdened with outmoded methods and tools?"

A hot flush spread across Laura's face, and she turned away, fussing with her hat. She was chagrined to be faced with the same argument she had used so often with her parents; it made her squirm inside to think she might appear as provincial and old-fashioned to Grant as her parents so often appeared to her.

"I agree with you," she said, looking at him at last. "My own family is burdened, as you say. We still use oil lamps, if you can credit it. Nothing I say will make my parents tap into the gas."

"Gas?" Grant cocked his head to one side and grinned. "They might as well not even bother—we'll all be using electricity for lights, soon enough."

Laura blushed yet again and the wind tugged at her hat, as though determined to pluck it off her head and blow it out of her reach. She glared at the water, both hands clamped down firmly on her hat.

"Then I suppose our newest hotel will be even more splendid than its name suggests," she said, pointing to a grand, bright-windowed building across the harbor. "It's called the Resplendent, and it's said to have every modern convenience."

"I guess it's easier to rig out the place in the most modern way if you start from scratch," Grant said. "Jack sure had the devil of a time getting the plumbing through that old Ship."

Laura narrowed her eyes against the glare and gazed out across the brilliant water at the Resplendent. It seemed to shine like a palace. "My friend Maggie is going to apply for a job there when they begin hiring. She thinks it's the smartest place to be, where everything is up and coming."

"Smart girl, your friend," Grant said, tipping his head to one side.

A boat went by at a clipping pace, and Laura felt a twinge of envy for Maggie, who was able to take advantage of such an opportunity. "I imagine every summer visitor will choose to stay at the Resplendent, from now on," she said wistfully.

"I wouldn't blame them," Grant agreed. "That's why Jack is so determined to modernize the Ship. You can't stand still and let the times pass you by. I'm all for the new."

"So am I," Laura said quietly.

She lowered her hands, sensing that the wind had died down. But before she knew it, another gust sprang up and snatched her hat off her head, hurling it into the harbor. Grant lunged to catch it, but too late.

"I'm very sorry," he said.

Laura watched the straw hat bobbing on the briny swells, and then let out a laugh. "I'm not," she said. "I don't know why I have to wear a hat anyway. If I tan, I tan. I've more important things to think about than just keeping my hat on my head."

"I suppose that makes you a modern woman," Grant said, eyeing the lavender in her hair with amusement.

Laura smiled, and turned her eyes back to the water where her hat was just sinking out of sight. "Maybe so."

Chapter Four

THE NEXT DAY was wash day at the Wild Rose. Daisy O'Roarke, the girl who usually came to help Laura and Mrs. MacKenzie, sent word that she was sick and could not work.

"Those Irish girls are always coming down with pellagra," Mrs. MacKenzie said, lowering the poorly written note to the kitchen table. "Now what'll we do?"

"The boys will have to help," Laura said. She tied on her apron as she strode out of the room. "But I'll have to catch them before they slip away to go berry picking."

Her footsteps echoed in the hallway. "Davy! Henry!" she called. "I need you!"

She paused, listening for an answer. The inn was quiet, its boarders and guests away on business, the tavern empty in the pale morning. Laura heard the old building creak around her, sighing like an old dog settling for a nap.

Then she caught a furtive sound that was not a house sound, but like two large mice hiding in the walls.

Laura listened hard, a smile spreading across her face. She tiptoed down the corridor, pausing where an old harpoon was mounted on the wall. Again she listened, and heard a faint scuffling.

In a flash she put her shoulder to the paneling. A hidden door swung inward, and Laura burst into a dusky, dusty passage.

"Caught you!" she cried.

A storm of protest and giggles came out of the dark. "How'd you know we were here?" David asked.

Laura took her brothers by the hands and drew them out of their hiding place. "I'd have to be as deaf as Mr. Ledue not to have heard you two galumphing around in there. What did you think you were up to?"

"We were smuggling," Henry explained as Laura pulled a cobweb off one of his ears.

"Smuggling what?"

The boys looked at each other in silence.

"We can tell her," David said at last.

Henry nodded, sober as a minister. "We were smuggling slaves. For the Overgrown Railroad."

"Good for you," Laura said with equal gravity. "That's an honorable family tradition. But you know, I believe that was called the Underground Railroad."

"It is the Underground Railroad," Henry said. "But our branch of it is covered with grass, so it's overgrown."

"I see." Laura fought hard not to laugh. "Now, boys, I need you in the overgrown backyard."

41

Before either one of them could turn tail and flee, Laura caught them both by the hand again and marched them outside.

"Daisy can't come today, so you have to help your poor sister with the laundry," she told them as she stopped at the pump.

"But that's girls' work," David wailed.

"I don't care whose work it is," Laura said. She placed Henry's hands on the pump handle and pushed a bucket under the spout. "You two boys get that water running for me."

"It's not right," David grumbled.

Laura watched a gull settle on a nearby roof. "Well, then, good-bye and fare thee well. Too bad I won't be able to tell you that story I read in last night's paper." She turned away to make the fire.

The boys were silent for a moment. They loved her stories, but were growing old enough to suspect when they were being bribed. Curiosity won out with David, however.

"What story?" he asked.

"I'm sorry, what was that?" Laura asked. She looked pointedly at the motionless pump handle.

Henry swung the squeaking handle up and down with a look that was half resignation, half expectation. Laura arranged kindling under the big wash kettle, turning away to hide her smile.

"The Trans-Mississippi Exhibition is going on in Omaha," she began in a storytelling voice. "That's in Nebraska, boys, way out West."

42

"Do they still have Comanches out there?" David broke in.

Laura frowned. "I'm not sure that's where the Comanches live. I think they're in Texas. It was Sioux in Nebraska, I believe, but I don't know everything. What I do know is that they have such wonderful things at the exhibition, you'd think you were in the Thousand and One Arabian Nights."

"What things?" Henry asked.

"Ohh, let's see," Laura mused. She frowned meaningfully at the boys, who were standing still by their full bucket of water. Together, they picked it up and sloshed it into the copper kettle, and ran back to the pump for more.

"The latest, most up-to-date telephones, for instance," she began.

"I've seen the telephone," Henry said with a narrow-eyed look. "They have it at the post office, Laura. That's not so special."

"Then what do you say about an X-ray machine that can take a photograph of your bones?" Laura asked. She reached out to tickle David's ribs. "While they're still inside of you?"

David burst into peals of laughter, but Henry shook his head, still unimpressed. "I wouldn't recognize anybody by just their bones. I'd have to see their outside parts."

"What's it for?" David asked, still giggling.

"A doctor might like to see where a bone was broken," Laura explained. "Without having to peel you like a potato to see inside."

"Nobody's going to peel me," David said grimly.

"What else do they have?" Henry asked. "Are the Handys going to get any of those inventions over at the Ship?"

Laura made a face. "Well, I don't know what the Handys might do, but I did hear the Resplendent has some of the very same things that are on display out there in Omaha," Laura said. "Like indoor toilets."

"Indoor?" David asked, his voice rising up in a squeak. "You mean like the ones you showed us in that catalog you keep in your room?"

"That's the very one," Laura said. "Imagine, not only is the toilet indoors, but the water washes everything away."

"Like this?" Henry picked up the bucket and poured out the last inch of water over David's head.

Laura screeched in surprise, and David let out a howl. In an instant, all three were chasing each other around the garden, laughing and trying to douse one another with buckets or dippers. Laura tripped over her hem and landed in a heap at her father's feet as he stepped out the back door.

"What is going on out here?" Mr. MacKenzie asked.

"I'm going to invent a machine that sprays people with root beer," David yelled.

"I'm going to invent a machine that turns silver into gold," shouted practical Henry.

Mr. MacKenzie watched in stony silence as Laura

44

picked herself up off the ground. "What happened to turn them into raving lunatics?" he asked. He was rubbing his left arm, a habit he had taken to, lately.

"I was telling them about the Trans-Mississippi," Laura explained, her good spirits trickling away under her father's stern eye. "I was telling them about some new inventions and we started—"

"Less foolishness and more work would be appreciated, Laura," Mr. MacKenzie interrupted. "Isn't it bad enough that Daisy isn't here to help? Can't the laundry get done with any sort of efficiency without your mother's guidance or mine?"

"I'm sorry, Father. It's just—"

"And stop getting the boys so riled up with crazy ideas," he added. "There's no sense making them dream of things that won't come true."

"But why not?" Laura lifted her chin, defiant and stubborn for her brothers' sakes and willing to face her father's bad temper. "Henry will inherit this place one day. Don't you wish to leave him a thriving business that he can manage into the nineteen hundreds? We're already so behind the times that nobody new wants to come here."

The boys stood nervously scuffling their feet as Mr. MacKenzie drew his brows together. Laura was afraid she had pushed her father too far and she held her breath, but then he let out a rich laugh.

"You think we're losing custom, Laura? I can hardly draw my breath as it is, your mother and me on our feet all day long with work that never ends. I've got a tingling in my arm that never goes away, I work so hard."

"But—" Laura bit off her words. It was useless to press the point that most inventions were laborsaving. Her father, once a cheerful, forgiving man, was growing more hard and impatient all the time, and it was clear that much was worrisome to him that hadn't bothered him before. Nor did she feel right about the sensation in his arm.

"Now, either put these boys to good work or send them away," Mr. MacKenzie said in a tired voice.

Laura glanced at her brothers. "Thanks for your help, boys, I can manage on my own, now."

Henry and David both turned and fled from the garden, not bothering to open the gate but clambering over the fence like two squirrels. A shower of rose petals fluttered to the ground as they went.

Laura watched her father watch his sons, and saw both pride and bleakness in his face. Their eyes met for a moment, and Laura felt a sudden surge of compassion for him and his hard lot.

"Father, don't you think you should see the doctor about that feeling in your arm?" she asked.

"No, no," he replied irritably. "Doctors just poke and pry so they can slap you with a bill, but they don't know anything. They're just a parcel of idiots."

Laura put her hand on his arm. "That's not so, and you know it. Dr. Merrivale is very up-to-date in his methods."

"Up-to-date, my foot," her father snorted. He

rubbed his arm again, his face drawn. Then he turned without another word and went back into the Wild Rose.

When the last piece of laundry had gone through the wringer and was clipped to the line, Laura sat down in the shade to fan herself. In the alley, the clip-clop of a horse's hooves echoed between buildings. The clopping stopped, and Laura heard Maggie's voice.

"I'll just be a blink, Pa."

"I'm in the garden, Maggie," Laura called out.

Maggie's cheerful face appeared around the corner. She was dressed in her new best dress, and there was a high color in her face.

"I need you, Laura MacKenzie, and if you turn me down I'll die."

"Then I'm all yours," Laura replied. She stood up and walked to the fence where her friend stood. Laura leaned over and saw Mr. Trelawney's ice wagon in the lane. "Hello, Mr. Trelawney."

"Let's get going, girls," he said. "I got ice melting here."

Walnut, the Trelawneys' horse, lifted one rear foot and rested it on edge, cocking its rump and swishing its tail at the flies. Mr. Trelawney had a habit of cracking nuts with his teeth and spitting the hulls at the horse, and as a result, the bay's rump was usually flecked with nutshells. Maggie took Laura by the hand, and the two of them climbed up on the seat beside Maggie's father.

"Hup," he said, flicking the reins over Walnut's back.

Maggie reached beneath her, pulled out a book she had sat upon, and shoved it under the bench as the wagon jerked forward. "I have to return that to the library," she said. "I expect I'll forget all about it, though, and Mrs. Millet is just waiting for a chance to dress me down."

"Is that the life-and-death mission I'm here on?" Laura asked.

Maggie tossed her head. "Of course not, you ninny. They're hiring at the Resplendent today, and everyone says there's going to be a scramble for the good jobs."

"Good job or bad, you'll take what's offered," Mr. Trelawney said tersely.

"Well, I might if it puts me in a good spot," Maggie retorted.

"You'll take it," Mr. Trelawney repeated, spitting a peanut shell at the bay.

In the presence of Maggie's father, the girls were too constrained to talk, but Laura was eager to tell her friend about Grant Van Doren. She waited impatiently as the ice wagon rumbled along behind the bay horse, leaving a trail of nutshells and water drops in the dust.

As soon as Mr. Trelawney stopped to deliver ice, Laura turned to Maggie.

"Do you remember that handsome fellow we saw at the concert the other night?" she asked, her eyes sparkling.

"Do I?" Maggie said. "Ask me something harder, like do I have two eyes in my head. What about him?"

Laura grinned. Typically, Maggie was the bearer of all news, but now the tables were turned. "*He's* Jack's cousin from New York. His name is Grant Van Doren and he's a student at Yale College and he's very charming."

Maggie's mouth formed a perfectly round O. "Well, you could knock me over."

"Where do you suppose Jack ever got a cousin like that?" Laura continued.

"That, I can tell you," Maggie said, settling back with a complacent look. "Louisa Carter told me everything—one of Jack's great-grandpa's sisters married a Manhattan Dutchman, who turned out to be Grant's great-uncle or some such thing. His father made a fortune putting in the new telegraph wires after the blizzard of eighty-eight. He's New York society, and he's *rrrrich.*"

Laura shook her head. "Here I thought I had one up on you, and you still know all the gossip."

"I may know the gossip, but you know Grant Van Doren," Maggie pointed out, eyeing Laura with speculation. "At least well enough to know he's charming," she added.

"We had a very interesting conversation," Laura said, wondering why she suddenly sounded so prim. "He has a very broad outlook."

"I take it you liked his company as much as his broad outlook?" Maggie teased.

Laura felt a blush sweep up her throat. "I don't

know what you're suggesting," she muttered as Mr. Trelawney came back toward the wagon.

"I'm not suggesting a thing," Maggie said. She examined her fingernails. "But as they say, it's just as easy to fall in love with a rich man as a poor one."

"Maggie, you sound so calculating!" Laura said. "Money should never be a consideration when it comes to love. And besides, what are we talking about love for? This is ridiculous."

"Hmmph," Mr. Trelawney grunted as he climbed aboard.

"Hmmph," Maggie said, her eyes twinkling.

They continued Mr. Trelawney's rounds, and the wagon made its plodding way out to Marblehead Neck. The wooded, rocky hump rising out of the water would have been an island but for the narrow spit that connected it to the mainland, and it was there that the wealthy had isolated themselves from the salty old town of Marblehead. The strip of beach beside the causeway was filled with bathers, children making sand castles, vendors selling ice cream, photographers for hire—hundreds of vacationers in a shrieking, laughing, splashing carnival.

But out on the Neck itself, all was quiet grace and restraint. On either side of the tarred road, large, elaborate vacation homes commanded vistas of either harbor or ocean, and close-clipped lawns lay smugly behind gates and fences. Laura and Maggie stared openmouthed as the Resplendent Hotel came into view.

"Isn't it just *grand*?" Maggie whispered.

Laura swallowed hard as they turned up the sweeping drive. The imposing hotel stood as though with its chin up, conscious of its own magnificence. Marble columns, broad verandas, and what seemed to be a thousand brilliant windows clothed the hotel in elegance.

"What do you suppose it looks like inside?" Maggie wondered aloud.

Mr. Trelawney spit another peanut shell at Walnut's rump and gave Maggie a warning look from under his brows. "Never mind what it looks like, Daughter. Mind your manners, take what they offer, and go in the service door!"

"Yes, Pa," Maggie said in a subdued tone.

The two girls climbed down from the bench, and Mr. Trelawney clucked to the horse.

"I'll be back after my rounds out here," he said in parting. "Settle your business and don't dawdle."

Laura and Maggie waited, arm in arm, as the ice wagon trundled down the drive. Then, as though a spell had broken, both girls turned with excitement to the hotel.

Chapter Five

LABORERS AND CRAFTSMEN were still busy about the place, and it was clear that more work was needed before the hotel was ready for business. The girls picked their way between stacks of bricks, past wheelbarrows, and squeezed between two wagons filled with potted palm trees whose flat fronds whispered together in the breeze. Four men shouted at one another as they struggled to move a grand piano through the doorway, and a harassed-looking foreman gave slow and careful instructions to some Italian masons.

"Where's the service entrance?" Maggie asked a bespattered painter as he ambled by.

"Round the side there," he said, jerking a thumb.

"I'll do anything to get a job here," Maggie said as they hurried along the veranda. "It's so modern!"

"It is," Laura agreed, her eyes on the chandeliers she could glimpse through the windows. "Do you suppose those are wired for electricity?"

"I hope so," Maggie said. "I feel like I'm wired up myself, I'm so excited. I just hope the housekeeper doing the interviewing isn't too much of a dragon."

With mounting apprehension, the girls entered the hotel by the service entrance. The corridor and vestibule were crowded with workmen and with people applying for jobs. As two men carrying a crate marked "Fragile" barged past Laura, she pressed herself flat against the wall and looked around. Even there, in the part of the hotel that guests would never see, the Resplendent was more elaborate than the best room at the Wild Rose.

"Maggie! Laura!"

They both turned in surprise. Louisa Carter and Abby Nightingale made their way toward them through the crowded hallway. Louisa grabbed Laura's hands.

"Isn't it thrilling?" she gushed. Two bright spots of color burned in her cheeks. "Isn't this the most elegant place?"

"I can't wait to look around," Laura agreed.

Abby was biting her fingernails and staring wide-eyed at the throng of people. "I never thought so many folks would come for the jobs," she quavered. "I sure hope I get something or my mother will tan my hide."

"I hope we all get jobs," Maggie said, stepping back as two more men carrying a crate barged through.

"I didn't know you'd be looking for work here, Laura," Louisa said, nervously fingering her hair. "Glory, what a crush!"

"I just came with Maggie," Laura began. "My parents need me at—"

53

"Attention! Quiet, please!"

An imperious voice cut through the babble and chatter, and the girls fell silent. Laura watched as a tall woman in a stiff black dress held up her hand for quiet.

"I can see that there are going to be many more applicants than we have positions to fill," the woman announced. "I will interview the female domestics one at a time."

"Oh," Abby moaned, closing her eyes. "I just know I won't be good enough."

"Hush up, Abby," Maggie said quickly. "Louisa, help me, my hair is falling down."

There was a general wave and rustle through the crowd as people straightened their backs and smoothed their garments or checked their letters of reference. Louisa turned Maggie smartly around and repinned her hair, while Abby wrung her hands.

Laura stood back, watching in silence as her friends prepared for their interviews. They were already far away from her, it seemed, about to walk down the hallway toward new prospects. Laura felt a twinge of regret that they were leaving her behind, but then she put those thoughts firmly out of her mind.

She slipped out of the crowd and wandered down a linoleum-floored hallway, peeking through doors as she passed. There were dayrooms for servants and for the head staff, an immense laundry, staircases and closets, gaslight in the corridors, and a persistent hum and bustle of activity throughout. The halls smelled of paint, plaster, wax, starch, and some new, sharp smell that Laura couldn't name but which she associated in her mind with progress.

Like a child in a fairy-tale castle, she pushed open a door at the end of the passage, stepped into a carpeted vestibule, and then rounded the corner. She gasped with surprise.

The main lobby of the hotel spread away from her like a ballroom. She stood transfixed as she gazed around her, oblivious to the hurry of workmen and the din of hammers and saws. The walls were covered with flocked paper, and the chandeliers were hung with a profusion of crystal prisms that threw off the sunlight in a scattering of rainbows. The reception desk was as grand and imposing as a judge's bench, and a trio of brass-caged elevators waited as though to transport hotel guests to heaven.

Laura wandered unnoticed through the lobby, gazing at everything as though in a carnival of delights. The hotel was like a machine, a fantastic conglomeration of moving parts that when operating smoothly would produce an experience called The Resplendent. Laura shook her head slowly, utterly impressed.

A door discreetly marked "Ladies' Convenience," swung open at her touch. Laura stepped inside, and for one startled moment, thought she had entered a roomful of people. But then she saw it was simply her own reflection thrown back at her from dozens of mirrors. With a smile, Laura tiptoed through the lounge, and then peeked through another door.

"A toilet!" With one quick backward glance, Laura

pulled the chain to make the toilet flush, and then laughed out loud at the sudden whoosh of water. Her laugh echoed off the marble walls, as though a crowd were enjoying the new sights with her. Then she wandered out to the magnificent lobby again and stood, just watching.

But despite her exhilaration, she felt an almost crushing sense of futility. The Wild Rose could never hope to compete with such modern splendor, even if it did try to keep up with the times.

"Laura!" came a frantic stage whisper.

Slowly, Laura turned. Maggie was standing at the edge of the lobby, beckoning urgently.

"Let's go!" she called.

"Come look at all this, Mag!" Laura exclaimed. "You won't believe your eyes."

"I'll settle for a report," Maggie said, darting in and dragging Laura back with her to the service wing. They raced down the corridor, their heels clicking on the linoleum. "That woman is a harpy, just as I feared, and if she catches me I'll lose my job before I even start! But I did get a job, that's the main thing!"

"Do you want to work here, if she's so awful?" Laura whispered.

Maggie slowed to a more demure pace as they rounded the corner and headed for the exit, which was still crowded by a line of applicants. "Of course," she whispered back. "Once this place opens it'll be chock-full of young handsome men. You can bet I don't aim to be a laundress all my life, and this is the best place to make sure I don't have to be."

Mr. Trelawney was just pulling into the drive as the girls emerged from the Resplendent, and they climbed up onto the seat beside him.

"Did you get a job?" Mr. Trelawney asked by way of greeting.

"Yes, Pa, in the laundry."

"It's a magnificent place," Laura said, steadying herself as the wagon jolted over a bump. "Elevators and chandeliers . . ."

"Hmmph," Mr. Trelawney said.

Laura and Maggie exchanged an understanding look. "I'll tell you all about it, later," Laura murmured to her.

When they reached town, Maggie stopped her father outside the dry-goods store. "I have to fetch some things," she told him. "I'll see you at home later."

"You might bring back some nuts, if Ledue has a good price," Trelawney told her.

"I will, Pa. Good-bye, Laura, I'll see you later too! You're a sweetheart for going with me." Maggie waved cheerfully as she hurried off.

Laura sat silently beside her friend's father as they went the rest of the way to the Wild Rose. "Thanks, Mr. Trelawney," she said, climbing down.

He gave her a brief, hard smile. "Surely. Might be a good thought for you to take a job out there, too, Laura."

"I've got a job here, though," Laura pointed out.

"Hmmmph."

Laura was about to turn away, when she caught sight of Maggie's library book under the seat.

"She forgot it," Laura said with a laugh, picking up the book. "Tell Maggie I'll return it for her."

She gave Walnut's flank a pat and then walked down the street toward the library, brushing a stray curl from her cheek. It was a warm day, and the sun draped itself across her shoulders like a cat. Laura smiled as she glanced at the title of Maggie's book: *The Countess of Craydon.* It was a very gothic romance, and Laura had enjoyed it herself. She let the book fall open in her hands, and reread a few lines to herself as she walked.

"Here's Laura."

She looked up, startled. Jack and Grant were coming toward her. Laura snapped the book shut and held it behind her.

"She's always reading something," Jack said in a bantering tone. "She's a crackerjack reader."

Grant smiled a greeting. "What is it today, philosophy? History? Or are you teaching yourself Italian so you can read *La Bohème*?"

Blushing, Laura shook her head. She was flattered by his guesses. "Oh, it's nothing."

While Laura was busy avoiding Grant's eyes, Jack lunged behind her and snatched the book away.

"No! Jack!"

He grinned and examined the spine. "Ooohoo! What have we here? *The Countess of Craydon?* It sounds very highbrow."

"It's not, and you know it," Laura said, glaring at

58

Jack and holding out her hand for the book. She glanced at Grant, fearful she might have slipped in his estimation. "And anyway, I was just returning it for a friend," she explained.

"I wouldn't have thought you would read something like that," Grant said.

Laura bit back a reply. She had read it, and she had enjoyed it. But for the moment, she was enjoying Grant's appraisal of her taste and sophistication. She stood, indecisive and feeling a bit like she had betrayed Maggie, while Jack riffled through the pages.

He began skimming the book, hooting with derision. "Listen to this—'The Countess staggered across the wind-ravaged heath, the porcelain-white skin of her hands bleeding from a profusion of—'"

"Oh, stop!" Laura cried, trying to grab the book.

Jack sidestepped away, holding the book out of her reach. "'The wind moaned across the embrasure of the tower,'" he continued to read. "Say, what's an embrasure, Laura?"

"It's a sort of window," Laura muttered. "Can I please have the book now?"

Jack's eyes widened. "But I'm just getting started."

"We all know such writing has limited merit," Grant broke in, deftly plucking the book from Jack's hand. "Don't bore us with a full recitation. I guess we're holding you up from doing a favor," he added to Laura as he handed her the gothic romance.

"No, that is—yes. I should be going," Laura said. She knew she was overly impressed and admiring of

Grant's gracious manners, but she felt a glow of pride that he counted her too discerning to read light romances. Laura also knew she wanted to earn his admiration. He seemed to personify everything that was new and coming, everything she wished to be.

"Good-bye, Laura," Jack said.

Laura barely heard him. She nodded at Grant. "Good-bye."

She walked on toward the library, resolving not to waste any more time on the *Countess of Craydon,* or any of the countess's sister heroines.

For three days, Laura did not see Grant at all, as she was too busy with chores at the Wild Rose both day and evening. Yet, as tired as she was when she closed her door each night, she kept the lamp burning for hours. She read the new books she'd taken from the library—works of the philosopher Nietzsche, and novels by Thomas Hardy and Henry James. In addition, she wrote feverishly and excitedly in her journal of all her ideas, and on Saturday night, she stayed up so late that she fell asleep with her head in her arms, propped up at her desk.

And yet she awoke early and refreshed, her mind already alive again to the possibilities of the day. She was eager for the chance to discuss new ideas with Grant.

But although it was Sunday, she still had obligations. Laura dressed quickly, and tiptoed down the hall past the doors of sleeping lodgers. In the kitchen, she stirred the coal stove to life, started a pot of coffee, and then set to work on a bushel of cucumbers. She had them chopped, doused with salt, and set to drain for the day on the back porch when her mother came in.

"I'm going to get Maggie to help me with these pickles later," Laura said, giving her mother a kiss. "Hers always taste so good."

Mrs. MacKenzie rubbed the sleep from her eyes. "Good idea. And I wonder if you'd stop up at Burial Hill after church. The family stones are overgrown."

"Of course," Laura replied. She slipped a pair of scissors in her pocket and went off to wrestle her brothers into their churchgoing clothes.

The sermon seemed to last all morning. Laura hardly listened though. She was too busy thinking of Grant. And as soon as the minister spoke his last words, Laura couldn't contain herself any longer. She ran out of the church and waited for Maggie.

"Come up to Burial Hill with me," she said, slipping her arm through her friend's as the churchgoers passed by them. "I promised to clean up some of our family markers."

Maggie rolled her eyes. "Oh, Laura. Why fuss over graves on a day like this? It's too pretty outside, and there's another concert at the bandshell and a military review."

"Well, I did promise," Laura pointed out.

"If you had any gumption you'd come with me," Maggie insisted.

"Gumption? I didn't know I needed gumption to listen to a concert."

Maggie shrugged one shoulder, and the sun gleamed on an old brooch at her throat. "I can't go alone," she said, pouting.

Laura shook her head, amused. "You just want someone standing at your side while you make eyes at the soldiers," she teased.

"I never thought you'd be so heartless."

"All right, then," Laura agreed. "If you promise to help me make pickles tonight, I'll meet you at the concert in half an hour. Is that a bargain?"

Maggie gave Laura a swift kiss on the cheek, her good humor restored. "I promise, honor bright. Now don't be long," she called, hurrying away.

Laura watched her disappear through the crowd, and then headed up the hill. The path wound among weathered gravestones that bore the names of Marblehead's past, and as Laura climbed among them, she felt a measure of satisfaction and security to have a place within such a long tradition.

At the top, she paused to look out over Marblehead. It was up there that Laura felt most keenly a sense of herself, a MacKenzie among the MacKenzies of the past. It was not a dragging, clinging past, but a foundation and a frame. Laura felt strong and tall and confident as she gazed out over the miles of ocean, as though she could cross the water in three long strides. All she need do was hitch up her skirts and step out.

"And fall right into the top of that tree," Laura chided herself.

She smiled at her own folly and turned to examine her family's markers.

Grant was strolling among the stones on the path below her. Laura's heart leaped with pleasure. She could hardly wait to talk to him again.

"Hello," Laura called out.

He smiled up at her uncertainly. "I hope I'm not intruding," he said as he took off his hat.

Laura was touched by his tact. "Not at all. I'm just here to clip a little grass." She smiled and held up the scissors she had taken from her pocket.

"If you mean to cut all the grass up here with those, you'll be all day," he said.

"Fortunately, I'm only responsible for a portion of it," Laura told him, laughing. She picked her way down the slope, and pointed to a stone beside him. "That's my grandfather Marcus you're standing on."

Grant stepped hastily to one side. "Pardon me."

"Don't worry," Laura said. The breeze blew a wisp of hair across her eyes, and she pulled it away as she knelt down to trim some grass. "He was a comfortable old man, and easy in his ways. So easy that few people suspected what he got up to."

"That's a provocative statement," Grant said, leaning against a Braxton marker and crossing his arms. "I'll take the bait: What did you grandfather get up to?"

"He hid runaway slaves in our house," Laura told

him. "But he was never caught—I think he took his cue from another ancestor, Matthew. He's over here."

Leading the way, Laura took Grant to a grave from a hundred years before, proud to have such a history to show him.

"Before the Revolution, Matthew was known as the mildest and most placating man in Marblehead, but all along his son John was smuggling rum and hiding it in the house. The British could never quite believe that Matthew MacKenzie was a desperate criminal," she concluded with a grin.

"Smuggling seems to run in the family," Grant observed.

"It appears that way, doesn't it?" Laura frowned thoughtfully at the lichen-covered stone. "But I think what runs in the family is independence. We make up our own minds, and act accordingly."

She looked up at Grant and was pleased to see him nod in approval.

"I suppose that could be said of the American character," he mused.

"Exactly!" Laura began to pace, her thoughts flying ahead. "And isn't that what we're seeing now? The great work is still ahead of us, and it's here in the United States that it's going to be done. Here is where the vital spark is."

"Our swift victory in Cuba certainly proves our superiority," Grant said.

"I'm glad the war was so short," Laura agreed. "There's so much more constructive work to be done."

"You're very forward looking."

"And yet you must also look back," Laura said. She gestured to the monuments around them, becoming more animated by the moment. "Whenever I read history I can never forget what my ancestors did. Think of the ones who came here first—when it was wilderness. They were bold and brave and ready to fight, and I am too." She rounded on him, her face glowing.

"Do you want to tame a wilderness, then?" Grant asked, plucking up a stem of timothy that she had cut. He chewed on the end of it and watched her expectantly.

Laura toyed with her scissors, a frown creasing her forehead. "I don't want to go West, or explore the poles or anything like that," she said. "I remember reading Thoreau—he says the frontiers are not east or west, north or south, but wherever we front facts. I want to *know* those facts. I want to meet them," she added vehemently.

Grant looked at her, a look of surprise on his handsome, narrow face. "You *are* independent. I can see I'll have to watch my step," he said. "And not just up here," he added, avoiding another grave.

"I don't think you have much to worry about from me," Laura replied, blushing with pleasure.

"You know history, you know literature, you know the modern painters."

"In that case, don't leave out political theory and mathematics and home economy," Laura broke in with a heady laugh. He made her feel that she was capable of anything. "I'm as sharp as a tack."

Grant grinned. "I can tell. Most of all, you seem to know your own mind."

Catching her breath, Laura knelt to clip the grass around a weatherworn stone. There, among her ancestors, her heart was telling her she had found a kindred spirit, a partner and equal who was as ready as she was to gather strength from the past and step ahead into the future. Her hands shook.

"I promised to meet a friend at the band shell," she said, raising her eyes at last to look at Grant again. "Would you—would you like to join us?"

"I'd be happy to," Grant said. "I expect I'll meet up with Jack there too."

"Then let me just finish here," Laura said hastily trimming more grass.

She heard him wander off and secretly watched him as he examined a headstone. His head was profiled against the brilliant blue of the sky. When he moved, she quickly ducked her head over her work again, impatient to be done. But while she worked, her skin seemed to tingle, her mind imagining Grant's blue eyes on her as she busied herself with the scissors.

"Done," she called at last, brushing the grass from her skirts.

He returned to her, holding out his arm for her to take. "On to the band shell," he said. "Marblehead seems to go in for music in a big way."

"We like our entertainments," Laura agreed. She felt proud and glad to put her hand on his arm. "There's also said to be a demonstration of some scientific apparatus today."

"Does that interest you?" Grant asked her.

They passed into the shade of an elm tree, and a robin called out loudly and sweetly as they went. Just then, Laura looked up at him, and her heart began to pound. For a moment, she couldn't think of a thing to say. He looked at her expectantly.

"The scientific demonstration?" he prompted. "It interests you?"

She came to her senses and nodded quickly. "It interests me very much," she managed to say.

He smiled. "You're an unusual girl, Laura MacKenzie."

As they walked out of the shade, Laura felt as though the light were filling her up. That someone like Grant was walking at her side seemed almost magical to her. He had appeared in Marblehead out of the blue, and the world suddenly seemed brighter and bigger, bristling with possibilities. She smiled to herself and glanced at him with a new sense of interest and excitement.

Grant began to tell her about a lecture on natural history he had attended, but Laura heard him with only half her attention. She wanted to listen, and to follow his conversation with intelligent questions and comments that would impress him and spark his continued admiration, but each time she looked at him she was thrown into a flutter. She couldn't imagine what had gotten into her.

As though in a dream, she walked at his side

67

through town, hardly noting what they passed even when they joined the crowd in the park overlooking the long harbor.

"Where is your friend?" Grant asked, pausing.

"My . . . oh . . ." Laura turned around, surprised to find herself among so many people. She looked around blankly.

"Laura, there you are!"

Flustered, Laura turned to greet Maggie. Grant took off his hat as Maggie ran to join them. The band was playing a march, the trumpets blaring with a jubilation that matched the brilliant sunshine.

"Well, hello," Maggie said, looking pointedly from Laura to Grant and back again. She smiled.

"Oh, Maggie Trelawney, may I introduce Grant Van Doren," Laura said. "We met up at Burial Hill."

"Hello again, Mr. Van Doren," Maggie said, dimpling.

"Please call me Grant, Miss Trelawney," he said with a bow.

"Only if you call me Maggie, as all my friends do," Maggie replied.

Laura wanted to drag her friend away and repeat every word that Grant had said to her. But she held herself back, too uncertain of what she was feeling to speak. She could hardly look at Grant, for fear that her confusing happiness and excitement showed too plainly in her face.

"I had no idea the graveyard was such a meeting spot," Maggie teased Laura.

"I met dozens of folks up there," Grant replied gallantly. "I'm sure I saw some Trelawneys."

Maggie swept one arm toward the concert crowd. "I hope you won't prefer their company to ours."

Grant laughed. "I couldn't possibly."

Laura knew she should speak, join in the bantering conversation, but she felt incapable of it. She needed to be alone to sort out her thoughts, and yet she didn't want to leave Grant's side. It was almost with relief that she saw Jack hail them and walk their way.

"How'd you get two girls, Grant?" Jack said with a laugh.

"Just lucky, I guess."

"Hey, there's a regular medicine show going on over there," Jack told the group with his usual brashness. "It's swell. They've got a galvanic sphere, and they're making all the girls shiver."

"That sounds exciting," Maggie said, glancing at Grant with a smile.

"I'm sure it is, but it's hardly a medicine show, Jack," Grant said. "There's some difference between electricity and snake oil."

"Not to me," Jack insisted. "Maybe I'm a simple fool, but I think it's all exciting—like a circus."

Laura blushed, embarrassed that Jack would boast of such a provincial outlook. And Maggie was biting her lip with pretended alarm.

"The electricity won't be dangerous, will it?" Maggie asked in a small voice.

"Of course not," Laura said with a trace of impatience. But she looked at Grant as she spoke. "Come. Let's take a look."

At one end of the park, a crowd had gathered around a platform on which a man in a striped suit stood lecturing. Before him was a metal sphere attached by wires to a hand-cranked generator. Children and grown-ups stood around in awe as the man spoke. Laura and her friends edged toward the front of the throng, and she stole a glance at Grant as he ushered her forward.

"Step right up, ladies and gentlemen, it's perfectly safe," the man announced. "The healthful and beneficial properties of electricity are thoroughly documented. The scientific heads of both continents are in complete agreement on that point."

"But what's it do?" Maggie asked Grant.

"The generator contains magnets and copper wire that spin around each other," Grant began to explain.

"And that creates a current," Laura broke in eagerly.

Grant smiled at her before turning back to Maggie. "That's right, you see—"

"Oh, I don't care how it works, it just seems like magic to me," Maggie said with a toss of her head.

"It's not magic, it's very real," Grant insisted. "You can feel the electricity if you touch the sphere."

"Oh, never!" Maggie cried, shrinking back in girlish alarm.

Grant laughed. "There's nothing to worry about."

"Try it," Laura urged. She stepped forward to prove it herself.

"That's right, young lady," the lecturer said, nodding to his assistant to crank the handle of the generator.

With a smile, Laura placed her hands on the metal sphere. Instantly, she felt the tingle of low current coursing up through her hands and throughout her body, prickling her scalp.

"Laura!" Maggie shrieked. She began to laugh. "Your hair!"

At the same moment, Laura felt the stray wisps of hair that had escaped from their pins rise up all around her head. Jack let out a hoot of laughter.

"Let me try that, too," he said, placing his hands on the globe.

Jack's straight red hair immediately stood out all around his head. Laura felt both ridiculous and happy, and threw Grant a look of pure elation. She felt she was touching the future.

"Watch out or your hair will stay that way, Jack," Maggie warned, stepping back with a smile. "I won't touch that invention for a hundred dollars."

Grant laughed indulgently. "It's quite safe, Maggie."

Laura took her hands away, but still felt the same ripple of excitement. "It feels wonderful," she breathed.

"It's crackerjack, really," Jack agreed, stepping away and smoothing down his hair. "Say, let's see if we can't find some lemonade, Grant."

"Why don't you two find a bench, and we'll get you some," Grant offered the girls.

Laura nodded, and as Grant and Jack walked away through the crowd, Maggie steered Laura to a bench.

71

"Can you believe he's real?" Maggie gasped, an expression of pure delight on her pretty face.

"No," Laura said.

Maggie leaned back and sighed. "He's like a hero stepping right out of a romance," she said. "He's so gallant."

"Yes," Laura murmured. "He certainly is."

She looked at her friend, strongly conscious of Maggie's naïveté, knowing that Grant had surely noticed it too. Laura suddenly felt she could not begin to explain the hodgepodge of feelings she had for Grant, doubting that Maggie could appreciate what their source was. For Maggie, the future meant having clever contraptions and a reliable husband to rescue her from drudgery. She wanted the future to pave a path for her. But Laura wanted to seize it and be a part of it, just as Grant did. But she could hardly explain her jumbled emotions to herself, let alone to her friend.

"And he's a college man too," Maggie said with admiration. "He must be smart as a whip."

"He is," Laura agreed. "I envy him that chance."

Maggie let out a peal of laughter. "Why don't you try college, then?" she joked.

Laura smiled. "Maybe I will," she said, pleasantly struck by a possibility that had never occurred to her before.

"Oh, saints preserve us," Maggie said in a broad Irish accent. She jumped up off the bench and pulled Laura's hand. "Now let's go see what's become of our lemonade."

Laura and Maggie linked arms and started across the lawn toward the lemonade vendor. The band struck up a waltz tune, and Laura and Maggie each executed a graceful turn as they went, and then laughed at their own giddiness.

"Now what's happened to those boys, do you suppose?" Maggie asked breathlessly.

Laura had already spotted Grant's blond head in the crowd. He and Jack were standing together in animated conversation, Jack holding two glasses of lemonade. While the girls approached, Jack made a wide gesture with his hands, sloshing lemonade onto the lawn. Grant laughed, clapped Jack on the back, and nodded.

"You look like a pair of conspirators," Maggie called out.

Startled, both Grant and Jack turned to see them. Neither of them spoke.

"My goodness," Laura said. "Now you really do look like you've been laying deep plans."

"They've been talking about us, you can rely on that," Maggie said to Laura with a wide-eyed, meaningful look.

"I wonder if they have," Laura said, sure that they had been.

"Actually Jack and I do have a plan," Grant said, "and you two feature in it."

Laura grinned, happier by the moment. "I hope you manage this plan better than Jack managed the lemonade."

"What? Oh, I'm sorry." Jack held out the two

glasses, which were both nearly empty. They all eyed the pitiful offerings with amusement.

"I hope you're not thirsty," Jack said.

Laura's eyes were on Grant. He looked as happy as she felt, and she could not stop smiling. "What is the plan?" she asked.

"A buggy ride out to the beach," Grant replied. He turned to smile at Maggie. "I hope you'll both say yes."

"A buggy ride!" Laura echoed with excitement. "What a wonderful idea!"

"I'm afraid Laura and I will have to have a consultation as to our social engagements," Maggie said in a tone of feigned regret. "You see, we're very much occupied this—"

Laura put one hand over Maggie's mouth and looked straight into Grant's eyes. "We accept."

Chapter Six

"JACK, SLOW DOWN!" Maggie called suddenly as the Handys' buggy jounced and rattled with a busy clatter along the crooked streets. She leaned forward with both hands on her hat. "You'll bounce us right out!"

"Don't worry, Mag," Jack replied. "I know what I'm doing."

"If the girls are frightened—" Grant began.

"Frightened!" Laura broke in, laughing. "It takes much more than Jack Handy to frighten me!"

The four of them had set out not long before, with Jack and Grant up in the driving seat and Maggie and Laura settled behind on the leather bench.

"Laura the Brave," Maggie teased. She leaned forward again between the boys. "But Jack, you might make your cousin think twice about staying on in Marblehead. If all he can expect is being tossed around like a package at the railroad station, he might want to get back to New York!"

Grant shook his head. "I'm in no hurry to leave, Maggie," he said, giving both girls a smile. "Believe me, I have every intention of staying on as long as I can."

Laura felt her heart give a little jump. To her relief, the road turned down a steep incline and the conversation was halted as they all watched Jack handle the high-stepping horse. The buggy bowled down to the narrow spit and Laura pressed one hand to her cheek to feel how flushed it was. As soon as Jack halted the buggy, Laura scrambled out ahead of the others so she could gather her scattered wits.

The sun blazed on the sand, and the curling waves were white with the reflected glare. Screeching, gleeful children and their Irish nursemaids romped in the water, couples strolled arm in arm along the strand, and the colored pennants on the concession stands snapped in the breeze. Out on the water, snow-white yachts plied the waves, and gulls beat steadily against the wind.

"Isn't it grand?" Laura asked, catching her breath as Grant came to her side.

"Beautiful day," he agreed. He looked back at Jack, who was tethering the horse Clinker to a flagpole. "Do you need a hand, Jack?" he asked, moving off to join his cousin.

Maggie stepped closer to Laura and linked arms. "He has the most elegant manners I ever saw," she whispered. "What a gentleman."

Laura nodded, her eyes on Grant's face, and when

he turned back to the girls, she felt a sudden onrush of exhilaration, as though she could do anything—jump up onto Clinker's back, turn cartwheels across the sand, sing all three acts of *La Bohème* at once while dancing a waltz and juggling swords—even thumb her nose at convention and go to college.

"Let's take a walk," Grant suggested.

"I'm all for that," Jack agreed. He came forward and unlinked Laura's arm from Maggie's, and appropriated Laura for himself. "Let's go."

"Now, just a moment, Jack," Laura protested, laughing and shaking her head. She glanced at Grant and then away, not wanting to be too obvious. "Who said you could make up the pairs?"

Jack gave her a crooked grin. "I look on this as a dance. The fellows always get to choose their partners at church socials."

"I'll go along with that reasoning," Grant agreed, offering his arm to Maggie and smiling.

Laura bit back another protest and submitted with good grace as Jack led her off across the hot sand. But she couldn't help looking back over her shoulder after a bit. Maggie and Grant were falling behind, talking and laughing and seemingly oblivious to everything around them. Laura wished desperately she knew what they were saying and wondered with a certain amount of self-satisfaction what Maggie would do if Grant tried to discuss history or politics with her. Just laugh, probably, and insist that she knew nothing about such things, Laura told herself drily.

Even as the disloyal thought crossed her mind, Laura stumbled over a pail that some child had left in the sand. Jack caught her arm to keep her from falling.

"If you want to walk backward, we can try that," he offered sarcastically. "I wouldn't want you to miss the view."

"I'm sorry," Laura said. She knew she was blushing, and that Jack knew why. "I just thought it might be more fun if all four of us could walk together."

"Maybe Grant would appreciate some conversation that didn't have him on the jump all the time," Jack hinted.

Laura let out an incredulous laugh and brushed a curl back from her forehead. "Jack, you don't understand your cousin at all."

"Maybe I know him better than you do," Jack said gently. "After all, he's my cousin."

Laura glanced over her shoulder again, confident that Grant would be glad to re-form the couples on the walk back to the buggy. As she looked yearningly at Grant, he raised his head and met her eyes. He smiled, nodded, and then politely gave his attention back to Maggie.

Laura turned forward, impatient but happy. She did not begrudge Maggie Grant's company: he had admitted he had every intention of staying on in Marblehead, and Laura was sure that she herself was the reason.

Before the jaunt had ended, Laura reminded Maggie about the pickles, and after supper, her friend strolled in through the back door of the Wild Rose.

"I can't think when I had more fun than I had this afternoon," Maggie said happily as she helped herself to an apron.

"I know," Laura said, almost to herself.

She set a canning kettle full of water on the stove and began dropping empty jars into it. Her mother was down the street, visiting with a sick neighbor, and the girls had the kitchen to themselves. It was warm and scented with coffee and ham from dinner. Laura felt a growing sense of excitement, as though she were a pot getting ready to boil. She bit her lip in anticipation while Maggie rummaged among the spice containers in a cupboard.

"I don't see any cloves!" Maggie warned. "How can I make pickles without . . . here they are."

Laura waited until Maggie turned around with her arms full of cinnamon, pepper, and allspice. At the expression on Laura's face, Maggie stopped dead in her tracks.

"What is it?" Maggie asked, eyes wide. "Something terrible's happened. I can tell."

"No, nothing terrible," Laura said, and glanced quickly at the door to the hallway. She looked back at Maggie again, beginning to grin. "I've made the most wonderful decision, and it's all thanks to you."

"What?"

"I want to go to college," Laura brought out in a rush.

Maggie gaped at her. "You what?"

"I want to go to college," Laura repeated, taking a step forward. "You said it yourself this afternoon, I should go to college."

"But I was joking!" Maggie's voice rose up in a wail. She set the canisters of pickling spice down on the table with a clatter. "What possible use is an education to a girl?"

"The same use it is to a man," Laura replied, bending down to retrieve the can of allspice that had rolled off the table.

"Oh, Laura, don't be naive," Maggie said. She busied herself with pots and pans and vinegar, a worried frown on her face. "Men need college because they go into important jobs and professions; they achieve things."

"So could I," Laura said mulishly. "I could have a profession. Just because women have seldom gone to college in the past, should that make the rule for the future? I thought you were interested in new ways of operating."

"What I see in the future is very clear," Maggie said, hands on her hips. "I'm going to better myself by marrying up. It didn't used to be possible, but it is now."

"But you're still only considering marriage as your only option," Laura said. "Don't you wish you had some other choices?"

"No, I don't," Maggie said with finality, rattling a

pot for emphasis. "I'm very happy to know just what's expected of me. I'll marry—well, I hope—and leave the choices to my husband."

Laura paced, as she always did when agitated. Her heels rang out hollowly on the wooden floor. "But Maggie, you're smart, I know you are."

"And I'll use what intelligence I have to pick the right husband," Maggie broke in. "If you're smart you'll do the same. I've seen plenty of old maids go out on daily work till they drop. That's what happens if you don't have a husband to protect and support you, and I am not going to let that happen to me."

"But it wouldn't," Laura protested. "You're so pretty, Maggie, any man would consider you a prize catch— don't you think being pretty *and* educated would make a woman that much more attractive?"

Maggie shook her head. "Don't waste your time with education, Laura. No man wants an educated wife."

"That's ridiculous," Laura scoffed.

"It is not," Maggie said stoutly. "If you went to college you'd be a bluestocking, and every man you meet will worry that you know more than he does."

"So you think men prefer women who know nothing except how to make pickles?"

Laura caught her breath and stared at Maggie, horrified by what she had said. Maggie set her jaw and turned away. In three long strides, Laura crossed the room to her friend and hugged her.

"I'm sorry, that was a terrible thing for me to say," she said, taking Maggie's hands. "Please forgive me."

"I forgive you," Maggie replied. "But in fact I think you're right, being pretty and making pickles are my qualifications. You can't enter the men's world—"

"But—"

"Laura, they won't allow you." Maggie's forehead wrinkled. "You'll only make them despise you, and they'll *never* want to marry you."

The scent of hot vinegar began to fill the room, stinging Laura's eyes. Laura knew her face was flushed from anger, from disappointment, and from fear. She was sure her friend couldn't be right; she had the evidence of Grant's admiration for her. What had been a wonderful and magical day was rapidly dissolving into frustration.

"Many things are changing," Laura said in a low voice, shaking peppercorns into the vinegar. "I don't know why this can't be one of them."

Maggie put one arm around Laura's waist and rested her head against Laura's. "Because men won't change," she said gently.

Suddenly, Laura pulled away, sick at heart. "So we're prisoners?" she asked. "Convention says we must find husbands and make good marriages, and if we stray from that we'll be punished? We'll end up scrubbing stairs and dying in the poorhouse?"

"I don't say I think it's fair," Maggie said with a frown. "I say it's the way of the world."

On the stove, the boiling jars were tapping and jiggling against one another, as though trying to get out of the hot water. Maggie poked at them with a knife, and attempted a lighthearted laugh. "And if you insist on being so contrary, Laura, no one will have you but Jack. He'll take you no matter what you do."

"That's not much comfort to me, I'm afraid," Laura said. "I don't love him, and I don't believe I ever will. When I marry it will be for love, and no other reason."

Maggie shrugged and pulled a jar out of the water with tongs, and Laura began to fill it with cucumber chunks.

"Love is a fairy tale, and it's beautiful to dream about, but I don't think it should be the only consideration," Maggie declared. "Jack's ridiculous sometimes, but he's going to do well with the Ship and he'll make a good husband. I might even try for him myself, but I know he's too taken with you to notice me at all."

Laura felt a deep sense of shock and sadness. In all the years that she and Maggie had been friends, she had never seen this hard and practical side before. It was as though Maggie had gained years of bitter experience when Laura was busy reading poetry.

"You really don't expect to marry for love?" Laura asked.

"Well . . . let's say I hope I'm smart enough to fall in love with a rich man," Maggie said. "And if you want to go to college *and* marry for love, then I'd have to say the pickle fumes are going to your head."

Laura could not help laughing, yet she felt subdued and disheartened and decided to let the unsettling subject drop. She was not at all convinced that Maggie was right, but she could see she'd never bring her friend around to her own point of view. They finished the pickles and talked of other, lighter things in preoccupied voices, and then cleaned up from their work.

"Let's get some beer," Laura suggested when the last utensil was washed. "I'm thirsty."

"I'll say yes to that," Maggie agreed.

There was a rift between them. Laura could feel disapproval and disquiet in Maggie's looks toward her, and Laura suspected that something had permanently altered in their friendship.

"Come on, then," she said with false brightness. Together, they went into the tavern, where a round of greetings paved their way in.

"Here's just what we need," Mr. Carter said. He turned from an obvious argument with three old men and appealed to Laura and Maggie. "Give us some musical refreshment, girls, you're our favorite duet."

"Hear, hear," chorused the familiar men.

Maggie dimpled at the crowd. "I can hardly sing with a dry throat," she told her father.

Trelawney grimaced and dug in his vest for some change, while Maggie gave Laura a wink. Maggie was all smiles, at the center of male attention, but Laura was still oppressed by her worries. Taking a glass of beer from her father, she went to sit at the piano.

"What'll you sing?" she asked her friend.

Maggie put her hand on Laura's shoulder, leaning forward to leaf through the pages of music-hall songs. With their two heads together, blond and brunette, they made a charming picture, as Laura judged by the indulgent smiles and nods of approval from the men around them. For a moment, she thought she would cry.

"Here." Maggie turned the page to one of her favorites, and Laura played the opening bars of "My Sweetheart's the Man in the Moon."

Maggie sang in a sweet, pure soprano, hands clasped in front of her, smiling at the audience. The men joined in on the chorus of the sentimental ballad, and from the corner of her eye, Laura could see her friend's animated face. For herself, she was glad her back was to the room, for she felt she couldn't smile. At the end of the last chorus, the group broke into good-natured applause.

"Give us 'Elsie From Chelsea'" boomed Mr. Hammond as Laura played the final cadence. "I do love that one."

"Certainly," Maggie agreed cheerfully.

Laura segued into the next song, and noticed the outside door open. Jack and Grant stepped into the tavern, shaking hands with the men nearest them. At once, Laura's spirits rose and she lifted her chin and struck the chords with all the artistry at her command. Maggie chose to sing Elsie in a Cockney accent, at which the crowd laughed and nudged each other in amusement. The lyrics were lighthearted, and the patrons at the Wild Rose ate it by the spoonful.

"Now, how about a song from Laura?" Jack called across the crowded tavern when the song was done.

"Oh, yes, you sing something," Maggie urged.

Laura was vaguely aware of smiles of encouragement around her. But her eyes sought Grant's where he stood by the bar. He raised his glass to her.

Emboldened, Laura put away the music-hall songs and spread the piano score for *La Bohème* in front of her. Her hands trembled slightly, but she kept her back straight. She had found a lovely waltz in the second act and had worked on it in odd moments. Now she cleared her throat, and found her way through the song, pronouncing the Italian as well as she could. The room fell silent around her as she sang, and Laura lost her nervousness in the sheer pleasure of the music.

At last, she lifted her hands from the keys, her face flushed with satisfaction.

And then the men behind her burst into astonished laughter. Shocked, Laura spun around on the stool to stare at her audience.

"But what's it mean?" Mr. Trelawney snorted. "I couldn't understand a word of it, Laura."

Laura rose from the piano, blushing crimson to the roots of her hair. "I don't know what it means," she admitted. "But I could enjoy it, anyway."

"How can you enjoy it if you don't know the sense of it, that's what I want to know," Mr. Ledue said, his eyes bulging. "It wasn't even in English."

"It was Italian," Mr. Carter explained. He smiled at Laura. "I enjoyed it very much, myself."

"Plain American has always been good enough for me, Mr. Carter," declared Mr. Ledue. His sharp nose quivered in indignation. "There's many a time I've gone into Boston and thought I'd stumbled upon the Tower of Babel."

Mr. Hammond nodded his heavy head. "I agree, Ledue. What with the Italians and Irish and Chinese and who all else—the place will soon be overrun with 'em. We'll have to look hard to find someone we can understand."

"*And* they're taking jobs away from Americans," Mr. MacKenzie said dourly. He rubbed his left arm with a gloomy scowl.

Laura gaped indignantly at her father. "But it was your choice to hire Daisy O'Roarke, Father."

"That's different," he insisted.

Mr. Carter held up his ink-stained hands. "Isn't there room in this great and vast country of ours for everyone who wants to work?"

"Sure," Jack said with a laugh. "Let 'em go out to Colorado or Utah."

Laura turned on him. "You don't mean that, Jack."

He just grinned, so Laura knew he was only trying to stir things up. "Stay out of it if you're just going to say foolish things," she warned. "We all of us are descended from people who came here from somewhere else," she added, turning back to the argument. "Why should we not—"

"Laura, Laura," Mr. MacKenzie said with a hushing gesture.

"I agree," Grant offered. "New blood revitalizes the body of the nation with new ideas, with innovations."

"Young man—"

"I'm of the opinion—"

The debate swirled around the room, and although Laura tried to join it, she found herself ignored by the debaters as tempers rose and backs were turned to her in the heat of argument. Laura was shut out and edged firmly out of the vortex of discussion. It was humiliating to feel invisible and voiceless when she knew she had so much to contribute. Even Grant had been caught up in the verbal tussle and seemed not to notice where she was.

Gritting her teeth, Laura turned away to hide the tears of frustration and disappointment. Maggie had been right the men would never welcome her into their sphere as an equal. They invited her only to provide entertainment, to be pretty and friendly and cheerful.

Maggie came to her side with a glass of beer, an indulgent smile on her face. "You certainly poked up a hornet's nest," she laughed.

"Damn them," Laura whispered, clenching her fists. "I won't be shut out."

Startled, Maggie lowered her glass. "What?"

Without answering, Laura shouldered her way across the room to the door, and hurried out into the street.

Chapter Seven

LAURA RAN THROUGH the gathering twilight. Many of the oldest streets did not yet have street lamps, but she could have found her way through Marblehead blindfolded. As she turned down a narrow alley, she paused to catch her breath, cursing the tight-laced corset that convention forced her to wear. A dog barked nearby, and a voice droned through a sanctimonious rebuke.

Laura steadied herself against a building, then turned onto a sloping street among the scent of pinks and marigolds. Before her was Miss Shaw's tiny house. She rapped sharply with the brass knocker and then stood on the granite step, gulping for air.

"Yes?" Miss Shaw opened the door, letting a stream of light pour onto Laura's face. "Laura MacKenzie, is that you?"

"Yes, Miss," Laura replied. "May I speak with you a moment?"

"Of course." The teacher led the way down a narrow apple-green hallway. Laura followed, aware of the scent of cinnamon, and the sound of her heels on the oilcloth runner. Her nerves seemed to vibrate like bowstrings. The teacher ushered Laura into her library.

"You smell of pickles, Laura. Please sit down."

Laura sat on the edge of a horsehair sofa, clenching her hands in her lap. Miss Shaw drew a chair close and sat back in it, the lamp casting her strong features into relief. Behind her, books sat squarely on shelves, and papers and pens and more books occupied the large desk. A case of geological specimens rested beside the articulated skeleton of a bat, and a framed watercolor of Salem's great harbor hung from the front of the bookcase. There was nothing tentative, nothing meek or temporary in the fixtures of Miss Shaw's private sanctuary. The woman sat very still, surrounded by the objects and products of her stern scholarship, waiting for Laura to speak.

"I hope I'm not disturbing you," Laura brought out at last.

Miss Shaw made a sharp, dismissing movement of one hand. "Not at all. Obviously something is disturbing you, however, and I assume it is something about which you need my advice."

"Yes," Laura agreed.

The two women looked at one another. Miss Shaw's clear gray eyes were neutral, without judgment. A garnet at her throat glowed bloodred in the lamplight. Surprisingly, Laura felt as though she might begin to weep.

"I need your help," she blurted out. "I can't bear the thought of—of—" Laura choked on her words.

"Of what?" Miss Shaw asked, frowning.

Laura pressed one hand to her chin to keep it from trembling. "Of disappearing. Of having no ideas. Of never wanting to know more than what I already know," she whispered. "I want to go to college."

To Laura's immense relief, her teacher's face relaxed into a warm smile.

"I'm so glad to hear you say that, Laura," Miss Shaw said. "I must admit, however, I never imagined your parents would propose that you go."

Laura felt a twisting behind her ribs. "They didn't propose it. It's my idea."

Miss Shaw nodded. A gray-striped cat slid out of the shadow beneath the desk and sat blinking up at her. "I see."

"Girls *can* go to college, can't they?" Laura faltered. Her legs were beginning to shake from suppressed tension, and she squeezed her knees together beneath clinging layers of petticoat and dress. "You went to college, I know you've spoken of it."

Miss Shaw rose from her chair and crossed the room, her long skirt whispering faintly in the quiet library. She adjusted the lamp to give more light.

"Yes, I went to Wellesley College when it was first opened."

"They accept women?" Laura asked.

Her teacher turned to smile at her. "They accept only women, and I don't doubt they would accept you.

You are highly qualified. Let me write to the dean and arrange for a place for you."

A flush of pride and excitement flooded Laura's face. She started up from the sofa, hands outstretched, and the cat darted out of sight. "You would do that for *me*?"

"Yes, Laura, I would," Miss Shaw replied in a surprisingly severe tone. "I would hate to see you—disappear, as you put it. It would be a brutal waste."

Laura felt a twinge of self-doubt. She was painfully conscious that she did smell of pickles, that her hands were stained by mustard seed, not ink. "I'm not a brilliant scholar, Miss Shaw. Please don't go to immense trouble on my account."

"Please don't dismiss yourself," her teacher said sternly. "You want to go to college, and I believe you should. I intend to do my utmost to see you get there. I have been your teacher for ten years; allow me to know what kind of scholar you are, Laura MacKenzie, and to know if it is worth my effort."

"Yes, Miss Shaw," Laura said with a strange mixture of embarrassment and elation. "Thank you. Thank you so much. I have many questions to ask you, but I'm so happy I can't sit still. May I come back tomorrow?"

Miss Shaw's face softened into a smile. "Certainly, Laura. We'll talk whenever you say. For now, good night."

Almost too elated to see where she was going, Laura hurried down the hallway and opened the door onto the street. The warm salt air touched her face, and a fingernail moon hung over the town like a handle just waiting to be grasped.

Laura stopped and gazed up at it. Many of her ancestors had been seafarers. For the first time, she felt as they must often have felt, embarking on a great voyage. With her heart hammering wildly inside her, Laura raced back through town and caught herself against the garden gate outside her house. She paused to recover her breath among the scent of roses.

As if in answer to an unformed wish, Grant stepped through the tavern door.

"It's you!" Laura gasped.

Grant walked toward her. "Laura? I was just coming to see if I could find you."

"You were?"

"Yes. I thought—well I hope you won't be offended, but I thought I'd offer to help you with the Italian, give you some advice about the pronunciation. You did a very good job, and I'm just sorry the audience didn't appreciate your effort."

"That's so kind of you," Laura whispered.

"Not at all."

As they moved quietly along the garden path, Laura felt as if she were rising into the air. Grant wanted to be with her, wanted to share himself and take her with him. If he was shy about saying why he sought her company, that only spoke louder and more eloquently. His manners had been sculpted by cultivated society, not roughened by the wind as the manners of Marblehead were.

"I'd be very happy for you to help me," Laura replied. Her skirts brushed against plants, letting out the hot sweet scents of carnation, marigold, and flowering tobacco. "And I have some wonderful news to tell you," she added, stopping to face him.

Grant clasped his hands behind his back. "Yes?"

"I've just been to see my former teacher," Laura began. She knew in her heart that Grant would be pleased and proud of her decision, but it was still so overwhelming that she had trouble bringing herself to tell him.

"And?" he prompted gently.

Laura drew a deep breath. "And she's going to find a place for me at Wellesley College," she brought out in a rush.

Laura waited for his answer. She heard her heart beat against her ears.

"Congratulations," Grant said at last. "You're a smart girl. You'll do well."

Laura let out a breathless laugh and turned down the path again. "So you're not one of those who think girls are good for nothing but marriage and mother-hood?"

"Not when they're as smart as you are."

Grant's words sent a vibration coursing through Laura, as strong as the electrical charge from the galvanic sphere. From the Wild Rose, the sound of the piano came faintly to her ears. Laura could not remember when she had been so happy. She laughed again, dangerously close to tears.

"I'm so glad to hear you say that," she whispered.

"You're a remarkable girl, Laura MacKenzie," Grant said in a quiet voice.

He stood facing her, and Laura suddenly wanted him to take her in his arms. She felt dizzy and swayed on her feet with the force of emotion. Grant caught her.

"Laura, are you faint?" he asked.

"No, no," Laura whispered, closing her eyes and feeling the warmth of his hands against her skin. She knew she had never felt this before, and knew that she was in love with him.

"Grant," she sighed.

"Laura, I want to tell you something."

She nodded, her heart brimming with joy. "Yes?"

The back door opened, throwing a wedge of light out into the garden. Startled, Laura stepped back and shielded her eyes.

"Laura, is that you?" Mrs. MacKenzie called. "Can you give me a hand inside?"

"Yes, Mother," Laura said reluctantly. "I must go," she added to Grant.

"Tomorrow, then," Grant said, holding out his hand. "We'll have our Italian lesson tomorrow and continue our private conversation."

Laura clasped his hand. "I'll find you at the Ship when I can get away. Good night."

He took his leave, and Laura drifted into the house, her senses throbbing. Mrs. MacKenzie was at work on the morning's bread. On the kitchen table, the jars of pickles that Laura and Maggie had made were cool enough to store.

"I'll take these out of your way," Laura said. She lifted two jars and carried them to the oven.

"Now there's an interesting plan," Mrs. MacKenzie said with a laugh.

"What? Oh!" Laura set the pickles down, grinning at her own folly. Her mother looked at her questioningly, and Laura only laughed with happiness.

Mr. MacKenzie walked into the kitchen. "This is a cheerful group," he said lightly.

"Laura's decided the oven's the place to keep pickles," Mrs. MacKenzie told him.

"Then I suppose I should look for my coffee in the cellar," Laura's father said.

"And your clothes in the barn," Laura added.

It was a rare treat to see both her parents so relaxed and smiling. It was yet one more delightful thing to have happened. Laura put her arms around her father.

"I have wonderful news," she said as she looked up into his face.

Mr. MacKenzie smiled and patted her cheek. "What's that, Laura dear?"

Laura held out one arm to include her mother in her expansive happiness. "Miss Shaw is going to find me a place at Wellesley."

Her parents did not speak. The mantel clock ticked busily into the silence.

"Is that another new hotel?" Mr. MacKenzie asked at last.

"No." Laura dropped her arms and her smile faltered. "No, Father, it's a college for women."

Mr. MacKenzie's face slowly darkened. "*That* Wellesley, where *she* went off to? What do you mean, she's finding you a job there?"

Mrs. MacKenzie began wiping her hands on her apron. She did not meet Laura's eyes.

Laura gritted her teeth. "No, Father. Miss Shaw is going to see that I attend the college as a student."

"A student? You think you can be a student at college?" he asked, his voice rising.

"Yes, I—"

"Absolutely not."

Laura quailed before his uncompromising tone, but held her ground. She raised her chin against her disappointment and frustration.

"Father, I am a good student. I have a good mind. I believe I can benefit from an education that does more than prepare me for housework."

Mr. MacKenzie was shaking his head. His face was red, and he began rubbing his left arm. Laura felt her heart drum dully against her ribs as she watched him. She knew she was dangerously close to tears, but she knew she had to fight.

"Women have no business going to college," her father said mulishly. He paced the kitchen, growing more and more agitated. "Getting notions, stirring up trouble. And most especially, Julia Shaw has no business to suggest—"

"Lemuel," Mrs. MacKenzie broke in.

Laura turned her head with a jerk, startled to hear her mother's voice. Mrs. MacKenzie was watching her husband with obvious anxiety. He was breathing hard, his face flushed with anger. Mrs. MacKenzie turned pleading eyes to Laura.

"Laura, we've no money for it," Mrs. MacKenzie said.

"And if we did have money for college, it'd go to David or Henry," Mr. MacKenzie thundered. He slammed his fist on the table, setting the pickle jars clicking against each other.

Laura heard a hollow tone in her ears, like the sound of the ocean in a shell, like a bell being broken. In her excitement, she had not considered the expense.

"And we need you here," Mrs. MacKenzie added. There was a bleak expression on her face when Laura looked at her.

"You need me here for what?" Laura challenged, looking from her mother to her father. "The way things are going there won't be a business for me to work at. You won't modernize, you don't encourage progress—I wonder you don't hold witch trials here! You're driving this business to ruin, Father!"

Mr. MacKenzie took two steps across the room and struck Laura across the face. She fell against a chair and it scooted out from beneath her. Laura clutched at the mantel, hanging her head, seeing stars. Her mind was white.

There was a horrified silence in the kitchen, broken only by the ragged sound of Mr. MacKenzie's breathing. He lowered himself into a chair at the table and dragged at the collar of his shirt, gulping for air. The next moment, he pushed himself up and away and stumbled from the kitchen, banging the door behind him.

Mrs. MacKenzie came close and cradled Laura's face, her hard, strong fingers smooth and cool against Laura's hot skin.

"Apologize to your father," Mrs. MacKenzie advised.

Tears sprang to Laura's eyes. "Me? I should apologize to him?"

"Laura, can't you see how it is with him?" Mrs. MacKenzie asked in a rising voice. Her lips trembled. "He's killing himself with worry. Don't add to it; please don't make it worse for him."

"So I must suffer along with him?" Laura asked harshly, her tears spilling down her cheeks. "Why should he be so angry that I want to improve myself?"

Her mother touched Laura's wet face with shaking fingers and shook her head. "Perhaps he sees you throwing yourself after an impossible desire, Laura. You must not yearn for what you can never have, you must not grasp at things which women never get."

"That's not true." Laura struggled to keep from crying. "Women can get what they grasp for if only others wouldn't drag at them and punish them for it. Miss Shaw did."

"Do you want to end up an old maid like her?" Mrs. MacKenzie asked.

"No! I don't know—" Laura broke away from her mother, her ears ringing. "*Must* I have a husband? Any old husband? Is that the sum of your ambitions for me?"

Mrs. MacKenzie's shoulders sagged. She carefully opened the clock and moved the long hand back five minutes as she did every night, as though by doing so she could erase what had just happened. "Laura, if you do not marry I will consider that a failure."

A sob rose in Laura's throat. She blundered out of the kitchen and through the dark hallway, dragging herself up the stairs. At the top she stopped to collect her thoughts. She should not have expected any different from her parents, she told herself dispiritedly. Yet their expectations of her still hurt.

Gathering her skirts in one hand, she climbed the narrow staircase to the attic where her brothers slept. A light showed under the door. Laura stepped softly and pushed the door open to see both boys asleep on Henry's bed, tumbled together like two puppies, and *Treasure Island* facedown on the floor.

There was a dull ache in Laura's heart as she knelt to pick up the book. Never to have a family of her own was a loss that Laura could not contemplate. But she would not believe—she refused to believe—that she must make an irreversible choice. Take one path, and she walked into darkness and a solitary existence; take the other, and she burdened herself with unrelieved domesticity.

"I can have both," she whispered, staring at the lamp and seeing Grant's face. Thinking of him gave her hope that she had another path open to her. She rubbed her stinging cheek, wishing with all her soul that it was Grant's hand caressing her.

Chapter Eight

AT THE MORNING'S first light, Laura kicked free of her covers and pulled a shawl around her shoulders. She swung the window wide, letting in the first dewy breath of the day, letting the flavor of Marblehead seep through her.

She knew she must recapture the sense of purpose and potential that she had found on Burial Hill, and that although Marblehead could make itself a prison for her, it was the only source of strength she had. It was her choice to make: her circumstances could be a millstone or an anchor. There was the ocean, both destroyer and giver of all riches the town had. There was the town itself, eccentric and old-fashioned, yet stubborn and independent. And here was her house, which consumed all her time and energy and yet sheltered her as it had sheltered the generations of MacKenzies. Laura leaned out to let the air touch her face, and felt the fringe of her shawl snag on something.

101

With a frown, she looked down to free it. The shawl was caught on an old nail that had slowly worked its way out of its bed. She pushed at it with her thumb and felt the whole board under the window slip at her touch.

As she pulled away the board, she could dimly make out some objects crammed in the space between the laths. She pulled them out and held them as the morning light strengthened.

A fragile bracelet braided of straw; a yellowed linen bundle that opened to reveal a carved wooden doll and an iron crucifix; these were the treasures the windowsill yielded. Laura examined them in wonder, turning the delicate bracelet over in her hands, rubbing her thumb across the doll's crude features, and holding the age-blackened cross up to the light by its chain. She felt the astonishment of discovery. Before her were relics of her own past, but she had no clues for deciphering them.

Laura closed her eyes, and bade her mind work, to delve into history and uncover the owner of these treasures.

With a gasp, Laura opened her eyes. "Bridie Mac-Kenzie," she said, suddenly as sure as if the doll and the cross had had her Scottish ancestor's name carved into them. Catholic Bridie had journeyed to the Massachusetts Bay Colony, strong in her faith, determined not to let the Puritans' rules subdue her. These treasures had been left by Bridie as stubborn monuments to her will.

The grass bracelet was harder to decipher, but Laura felt sure that it was a love token. Why else save such a delicate wreath, such an ephemeral and unwearable plait? Some other ancestor had placed it there, as though keeping her heart secure.

Laura felt an upwelling inside her, and the sun poured through her window, onto the signs from the past. She could not help smiling.

She could not wait to see Grant. It would all come right. Laura knew she would make her way to college, and Grant would be at her side, encouraging her, applauding her, loving her. There was no way to fail, not with such models of determination as she held in her hands.

With growing confidence, Laura replaced the doll and the cross and the grass bracelet in their cranny. Then, taking her journal from her desk, she sat at the window and poured her thoughts into it, her hand racing across the pages with the urgency of her hopes and her desires until a nearby clock struck seven.

Hurriedly, she dressed and raced through her morning's chores, careful to avoid her parents. She was determined not to let their old-fashioned prejudices cloud her happiness. As soon as she could, she made her way to the Ship.

Jack was just walking out the door and he immediately linked her arm through his and turned her away from the house.

"Good morning, Laura, beautiful day, isn't it?" he said.

"Not so fast," Laura replied. She extricated herself from him, less patient than ever with Jack's gallantries, and hopped up on a mounting block to slip around him.

103

But Jack barred her way. He grinned and ran a hand through his hair. "I wonder if you can settle an argument we had here last night."

Laura suppressed a sigh and glanced over his shoulder at the door of the Handy's hotel. It was maddening not to be able to see Grant. "Yes, what is it?"

"Oh, um, it's about the—the—" Jack made a face and barred Laura's way yet again as she stepped down and tried to head for the door. "About the Marblehead Society for the Beautification and Preservation of the Graves of the Glorious War Dead. Say, that's a new dress, isn't it?"

"No, it's not a new dress," Laura retorted. "Of all the silly excuses for getting my attention, Jack, honestly. What possible interest do you have in the graves of the glorious war dead?"

A pained expression crossed his face. "Well, you know my uncle Micah Handy fell at Gettysburg."

Laura felt her cheeks redden. She watched a fisherman clump past in his heavy sea boots, a bucket of clams in one hand. Water sloshed over the rim of the bucket, splotching the dirt.

"I know," Laura said. "I'm sorry, Jack. It's just that I particularly wanted to speak to Grant."

"Grant?" Jack asked with a sheepish look. He looked back at the door and chewed on his lower lip. "Umm . . . he's not precisely here . . ."

"Whatever do you mean? Is he here, or isn't he?" Laura asked, holding her temper with difficulty. She strode to the door of the Ship and grasped the polished knob.

Jack didn't answer. He kicked at a lump of horse manure, a ferocious scowl pulling his face awry. It was obvious that he didn't want her to see Grant, and although it was irritating, Laura was touched by his jealousy.

"Jack?" Laura asked more gently.

"Yes, he's here," Jack said. He raised anxious eyes to her face. "Only—don't go in. Come for a walk with me instead."

Laura shook her head. "No, Jack. I'm sorry." She was truly sorry if he was hurt by her bond with his cousin. But she had never made any promises to Jack, and any illusions he had were of his own making.

She strode through the house, peeking into the parlors and smoking rooms. The Handys' housemaid, Marianne, was scrubbing the stairs.

"Have you seen Mr. Van Doren, Marianne?" Laura asked.

"That la-di-da fellow from New York City?" Marianne grumbled. She jerked her head. "Out back in the garden."

There was a tread on the floorboards behind Laura. She turned her head. Jack had followed her in.

"Laura, trust me. Don't ask why, just please don't go."

"Don't be ridiculous," Laura said impatiently. She ran lightly down the hallway to the door giving on the

105

back garden. The latch stuck as she struggled with it. Everything seemed to thwart her.

At last, she swung the door wide and the bright garden opened before her like a stage set. And just as if it were a scene in a romance, a couple stood under a twisted oak tree, holding hands, their heads bent together. Grant and Maggie.

Laura blinked, wondering if Maggie had a splinter in her palm that Grant was trying to remove. Then, as Laura stood mutely on the doorstep, Grant whispered something in Maggie's ear, and Maggie let out a laugh that rang like a chime from the dappled shade.

A sickening jolt rocketed through Laura's blood. Turning, she stumbled back into the dark hallway, blundering past Jack.

"Laura, I—"

"No," she gasped. She made a cutting motion with one hand, and ducking her head, ran out of the Ship.

As she burst through the door, she found herself enmeshed in a shouting match. Two wagons had met head-on in the narrow street, and neither driver would back up his team. A crowd had gathered, choosing sides like spectators at a prizefight, and Laura could not find a path through the shouting throng.

"Back up your animals!" cried the Italian driver of a grocery wagon, standing up and gesturing with his reins.

"Back up yourself, you foreigner," shouted the driver of the town manure wagon.

"Me, I am an American good as you!" the Italian declared roundly.

Several people offered advice, and one boy snuck a carrot from the back of the grocery wagon. Both teams of horses stood patiently whisking their tails, unconcerned. With mounting frustration, Laura tried to slip through a gap in the bodies, but a bricklayer stepped onto her foot. Laura let out a yelp of pain, and tears sprang to her eyes. The Italian driver began a rousing recital of abuse in his native tongue.

"This is quite a melodrama," Grant said from behind her. "I could hear them all the way in the garden."

Laura's heart jolted painfully at the sound of his voice, and she could not look at him. She ducked her face away in anguish, and hastily wiped away the welling tears. "Yes," she gasped.

"Did you come for your Italian lesson? If so, it's wonderful timing. The grocer is calling the manure collector a son of a drunken Sicilian," Grant said, amused. "Which must be a pretty dreadful insult, judging by how smug he looks."

"Yes, I'm sure." Laura was trembling. She could not believe she had been such a fool, that she had imagined Grant loved her. She could not believe he was still speaking to her, in the same tone as always, unaware that the ground was falling away beneath her feet.

"Why, Laura, are you crying?" Grant asked, his voice filled with concern.

"No—yes—someone stamped on my foot," Laura whispered. She dashed away the tears and steeled herself to look at him. What she saw in his eyes was friendship and respect, nothing more. "I'm fine."

"Come, let's get out of this ridiculous brawl," Grant said, taking her arm and steering her toward the edge of the crowd.

Laura followed blindly, unable to think or speak. She was utterly miserable. She, who had prided herself on such wisdom and intelligence and insight, had built an elaborate fantasy out of nothing. She was a fool.

"When I offered to teach you Italian I didn't know you would have the genuine article to listen to," Grant observed as they left the argument behind.

"No, I don't suppose you did," Laura said with difficulty.

She tripped over a cobble. Grant steadied her, and although Laura recoiled from his touch, he seemed not to notice. He drew a deep, appreciative breath. "It's a beautiful day, isn't it? *Un bello giorno.*"

"Yes," Laura said, looking dully at the ground. She made herself smile. She could not let him know what she had imagined. "It's a beautiful day."

Grant smiled widely, and they continued walking. He walked at a brisk pace, and every movement of his body showed that he was agitated, almost exhilarated. Laura was sickeningly sure of why he seemed ready to burst into song, or about to jump into the air and click his heels: she herself had felt the same way just yesterday.

"Laura, forgive me if I sound foolish, but I feel I can confide in you, there's such a free communication between us," Grant began in a hesitant voice. "I wanted to tell you last night, but we were interrupted."

"Yes?" Laura asked. She dreaded hearing him go on.

They stopped at the harbor, and Grant stood with his hat in his hands, the breeze toying with his hair. A fishing boat was unloading crates of fish, the skins gleaming black and silver. Gulls shrieked overhead, clamoring for the catch.

"Laura, I want to thank you for introducing me to Maggie," Grant said with a disarming smile. "She's a grand girl."

Laura looked away and fixed her eyes on the soot-stained funnel of the fishing boat. Her head was beginning to pound. "Yes, Maggie's a very grand girl," she agreed softly. "I love her dearly."

"She's so charmingly simple and naive," Grant continued. "There's a freshness to her, a wholesomeness that you don't find in the girls in New York, believe me."

"I believe you," Laura whispered.

"And she's so full of innocence. Many girls pretend it, but she's the genuine article—the way she shrank from the electrical demonstration was the sweetest thing I ever saw. And our trip to the beach was the most wonderful afternoon of my life."

Every word wounded Laura worse than the last. The breeze gusted across her flaming cheeks and drove strands of hair into her stinging eyes. She wished she could tell Grant to stop, but she could not speak. On the boat, the fishermen were swapping bawdy jokes about President McKinley's plan to annex Hawaii. Laura knew about Hawaii, had even read a biography of its overthrown monarchy. She was beginning to wish she had never read anything at all.

Grant began to pace. "Last night, when she was singing at the piano," he went on with a love-struck laugh, "those songs she chose were so quaint, so delightful—it was like listening to the voice of a flower."

"What a sweet thing to say," Laura murmured, her heart wrenching inside her.

She wanted to turn and scream at Grant, to say spiteful and traitorous things about Maggie. But she couldn't. Maggie's vivacious spirit had captured Grant's heart; Laura's eager curiosity and questing mind had only won his confidence and respect.

"Well, enough romantic bosh," Grant said, laughing again self-consciously. "How about that Italian lesson?"

"I'm sorry," Laura said. She had to control her voice very carefully to keep it from breaking. "But my head aches terribly."

"Oh, I'm sorry." Grant ran his hat brim through his fingers. "Perhaps later, then."

Laura nodded, turning quickly away. "Yes, that would be better."

Grant paused for a moment. Then he put his hat on. "I hope you'll be well soon," he said sincerely.

Laura stood rigidly, staring out at the harbor with its crossing ships and snapping flags as Grant's footsteps receded. The boats and yachts passed back and forth across her vision, their crews as faraway and unreachable as men on the moon. Laura bent her head, covering her

110

face with her hands. She stood there for several minutes, trying without success to empty her mind.

"Laura?"

At the sound of Jack's voice, she spun around and faced him bleakly. "Jack, you knew. Why didn't you stop me?"

"I tried to," he reminded her.

With a sob, she buried her face in his shoulder, and he put his arms around her. "I thought he loved me," she cried. "But he never considered me at all."

"There, there," Jack said helplessly.

Laura shook her head, her tears hot on her face. "I'm such a fool," she said, gripping Jack's shirtsleeve. "Maggie was right—no man wants an intelligent, educated woman."

"I do," Jack said.

Laura pulled back and let out a tearful laugh as she met his eyes. "Jack, you're so good," she said, touching his cheek.

Jack took her hand and kissed it. "I love you, Laura. You know I do."

"I know."

Laura closed her eyes, but all she saw was Grant's face. "I know," she repeated as tears spilled over her cheeks again. "But—"

"But you don't love me."

Gently, tearfully, Laura pulled her hand away from Jack's, all too familiar with what he felt. "You're so loyal and good to me," she said, looking down. She saw one of her own tears splash in the dust between them. "I value your friendship more than gold, Jack, I truly do."

"I guess I have to be satisfied with that then, don't I?" he replied hoarsely.

Without looking up, Laura nodded, and then turned her steps toward home.

Chapter Nine

LAURA WALKED INTO the Wild Rose, shut the door carefully behind her, and stood with her back against it. She faced the empty tavern. The room smelled faintly of pipe smoke, and the worn floorboards gave off their old, musty scent of beer and briny boots.

As she stood there, lost in thought, the opposite door opened and Henry darted in, a half-eaten muffin clutched in his hand. He skidded to a halt when he saw her.

"Miss Shaw's here," he whispered, his eyes wide. "I'm cutting out. She might want to quiz somebody, and it's not going to be me."

Without speaking, Laura stepped aside and let her little brother escape. Then she crossed the tavern, and went out into the corridor, where she heard the murmur of voices from the parlor. She walked toward them, knowing that she herself was the subject of discussion.

Her parents and Miss Shaw all looked her way as Laura opened the door.

"Good morning, Laura," Miss Shaw said. She sat ramrod straight in her chair, a cup of tea balanced in one hand.

"Good morning," Laura said quietly.

The adults turned back to their discussion. Mr. MacKenzie's mouth was set in a stern line and his nostrils were pinched. "Miss Shaw, I tell you again for the last time—"

"I heard you the first time and the second time," Miss Shaw interrupted, her eyes hard. "Lemuel MacKenzie, I have heard you, but I don't believe you have heard me. Laura is cut out for more than a serving maid and mother, and you should recognize that."

Mrs. MacKenzie went pale at the implied insult to herself. "She could do worse than that," she said proudly.

"Martha, I know, forgive me," Miss Shaw said, quickly turning to Laura's mother. "But you know as well as I do that she can do so much better."

"Pardon me, Miss, but what Laura does is none of your affair," Mr. MacKenzie said with growing anger.

"I think it is," Miss Shaw insisted, uncowed. "If you are as determined to stand in your daughter's way and thwart her ambitions as you were to thwart mine—"

"That's in the past," Mr. MacKenzie said, his face flushing. "But I expect you put her up to this, for that matter."

"I guessed you would think so, so I never suggested

114

it to Laura," Miss Shaw replied in a voice taut with suppressed anger. "She came to me of her own accord."

"Please . . ." Laura spoke up at last, and her elders looked at her in surprise. She didn't understand what bad blood was between her father and Miss Shaw, but they were locking horns for no purpose. "Miss Shaw, perhaps I don't wish to go to college as much as I thought."

Her teacher drew her breath in sharply, and Mr. MacKenzie threw Miss Shaw a triumphant look. Mrs. MacKenzie gave a small shake of her head.

Laura twined her fingers together, and then broke her hands apart, as though she didn't know what to do with them. She was all at odds with herself. She wished she could go to sleep. There was no place for her anywhere.

"Miss Shaw, last night I was enthralled by a notion that—that—" Laura fought for words. "Perhaps I spoke without thinking."

Her teacher looked at her with a speculative expression in her cool gray eyes. "Perhaps you did, but that does not mean it was not the truth."

Laura gulped, and looked pleadingly at her mother. Mrs. MacKenzie held out her hand, and Laura clung to it. After her disappointment, she could not help seeing Miss Shaw as a single woman, as sharp and bristling with her independence as a porcupine. Miss Shaw had embraced the life of the mind and ended up with a spinster's empty bed.

While Mr. MacKenzie folded his arms across his

chest and glowered, Miss Shaw gathered her umbrella and her handbag and stood up.

"See Miss Shaw out," Mrs. MacKenzie said quietly, pushing Laura away.

Mr. MacKenzie looked as though he wanted to object, but he strode across the room and turned his back to them all.

Hanging her head, Laura preceded Miss Shaw from the parlor and walked down the long, echoing hall to the tavern door. On either side, oil paintings and photographs of MacKenzie ancestors and sailing ships were like two rows of watching sentries. Laura opened the door and stood aside to let her teacher pass through.

"There's still time to reconsider, Laura," Miss Shaw said.

"I don't know that I will," Laura said, not meeting her teacher's eyes. She crossed the empty taproom and held open the outside door. A bicycle bell rang down the street. "There's no money, even if I did," she added quietly.

Miss Shaw stood where she was, unmoving until Laura raised her eyes and looked at her. Her teacher's face showed obvious dismay. Outside on the street, an automobile put-putted by, but neither of them turned to watch it.

"Laura, what happened?" the woman asked gently.

A hard lump formed in Laura's throat. She shook her head, unable to speak. Dust from the passing auto settled onto the doorstep.

"Very well." Miss Shaw walked past her, but paused on the threshhold. "Come talk to me when you can."

Laura couldn't answer. She watched as Miss Shaw went out into the street. Mr. Carter, stepping out of the newspaper office, called out to the teacher, and the two went back inside the office together. Laura closed the door.

"Well, of all the effrontery," her father exploded. He had come into the tavern behind her. "Interfering old busybody. That woman has no business poking into our family affairs."

"She only means to be kind, Father," Laura said, hurt for her teacher's sake. "Besides, she went to college, so she speaks from experience."

He made a face. "Hmmph. And you want her experience? She was never a beauty, like you are. It's no wonder she had to rely on her wits, and she has only herself to blame for throwing away what was offered. I've no doubt she's jealous of you."

"Jealous?"

"Yes, jealous," he insisted, rubbing his arm. "It's only natural, seeing as how she ended up an old maid. Now she wants to make you one too."

Laura stared at her father in disbelief. "How can you speak so unjustly? She's done well by her education and wants as much for me."

"Education—I never went to college," Mr. MacKenzie grumbled. "She's jealous, mark my words."

Laura sighed, suddenly more tired than ever. "Don't

worry, Father," Laura said in a dejected voice. She brushed past him. "I know I am not going to college."

"As if you really wanted to," he said smugly.

Laura looked back at him, hurt and baffled that he felt as he did. "But wouldn't you be proud of me if I did?" she asked.

Her father blinked. "Why, I am proud of you already, Laura. You're a beautiful girl. All the more reason not to ruin your looks poring over books and—"

"Let's not talk about it any longer," Laura begged.

He stepped behind the bar and began polishing glasses. "That suits me down to the ground. We'll hear no more on the subject."

Laura nodded. "Yes, Father," she said, and left the room.

For two days, Laura tried to put all thoughts of college, and of Grant, behind her. Each was equally unattainable, and though it grieved her, Laura tried to resign herself. The ambitious stack of library books on her desk remained untouched, and she dared not open her journal, for fear of unlocking floodgates of regret. She stayed close to home, and applied herself with a vengeance to the chores most suited to her station—a station about which she had no choice.

Yet her sleep was troubled, and after a second restless night, she awoke tired and dark-eyed with weariness. She moved through the kitchen like an automaton, heating water to take to the lodgers' rooms. Mrs. Mac-Kenzie, stoking the stove, eyed Laura with concern.

"You look so peaked, Laura," her mother said. She pressed one hand to Laura's cheeks. "Maybe you should take some of that tonic I bought last week."

"I don't need a tonic," Laura replied.

The boys clattered into the kitchen, tucking in their shirts and dragging their bootlaces. Henry put a jar with a butterfly in it on the table as he sat down.

"Is there any more of that pie you made yesterday, Laura?" David asked. "I love pie for breakfast."

"No, it's all gone," Laura answered distantly.

"It was a good pie, dear," Mrs. MacKenzie said. "Really it was better than any you've ever done."

Laura began beating pancake batter, letting her breath out tightly. "I'm glad to hear you say that," she said with some irony.

"What kind of butterfly is this?" Henry asked, holding the jar up for Laura's inspection.

She didn't glance at it. "I don't know," she replied.

"Can't you guess?" Henry urged. "You've guessed before."

"Well maybe I'm through with butterflies," Laura said sharply. She saw Henry's face fall, and she touched his shoulder with a light hand. "I'm sorry. You'll have to look it up."

The boys were noisy over their breakfasts, arguing about the relative merits of haddock or cod for attracting flies, and drumming their heels against the chair rungs. Mrs. MacKenzie and Laura prepared breakfast for their

119

boarders, moving about one another with familiar efficiency. Laura was conscious that her mother kept looking at her, but Laura avoided her mother's gaze.

But finally, when wash water was lugged upstairs, and breakfast had been served in the dining room, and the morning's dishes washed up, Mrs. MacKenzie took Laura's arms and made her face her.

"What is it, Laura?" her mother asked. "You haven't been yourself, the last few days."

"Yes, I have," Laura muttered. She toyed with her mother's apron, wishing she were a small child again.

"You've been working in the garden, making pies, scrubbing floors—it's not like you."

Laura let out a rueful laugh. "You mean it's not like me to work?"

"No, that's not it," Mrs. MacKenzie said. "But there's a change in you."

"I'm fulfilling my role in life," Laura said in a brittle voice. "Isn't that what you want me to do?"

Mrs. MacKenzie smoothed Laura's blond hair, her eyes troubled. "Yes. I think it's best. But I want you to be happy too."

"I never had the impression that happiness was something I could expect, Mother," Laura said.

"I'm happy," Mrs. MacKenzie told her.

"Are you?" Laura gripped her mother's hands tightly, and searched her mother's face. "Are you, Mother? You work so hard, and Father's often so cross, and there's no money, nothing but work work work."

"I have my children," Mrs. MacKenzie said.

"You have your sons." Laura's throat hurt her to say it.

Mrs. MacKenzie shook her head. "I have my daughter, my shining, golden daughter," she said. "Who is everything I never was."

Laura felt tears come to her eyes. "Mother?"

"I want everything good for you," Mrs. MacKenzie said in an emotional voice. "If only we did have the money, I would give you anything you asked for."

"What do you mean?" Laura gripped her mother's hands tighter. "Mother, are you saying you'd want me to go to college? Is that it?"

Mrs. MacKenzie sighed heavily. "It's not to be, my dear. Try to make a good marriage."

"Oh!" Laura broke away, crossing the kitchen with an angry step. She clenched her fists at her sides, trying to quell the resentment that kept threatening to overwhelm her. She was afraid she would turn hard and dry and sour, like a lemon left on a shelf.

"Perhaps you're right, Mother," she said in a tight voice. "I should apply myself to becoming marriageable."

Her vision blurred momentarily with tears. Sniffing hard, she yanked open the kitchen door, and went out to the garden. From the shed she took twine and a knife, and applied herself to tending the roses that sprawled across the fence and gate.

The hardy stalks fought with her as she strove to tie them into place, and the thorns hiding among the glorious blossoms scratched at Laura's arms. One thorn jabbed the ball of her thumb and Laura yanked her hand away, her heart hammering with alarm at how quickly pain came crowding around her.

"Laura!"

She looked up at the familiar voice, her face stricken.

Maggie ran toward her down the street, waving eagerly. "I've been dying to see you!"

Laura stood sucking at the blood on her thumb as Maggie danced up. She lowered her eyes when she saw the sparkle in Maggie's.

"Pricked yourself with a thorn?" Maggie asked. She leaned on the fence and let her feet dance a dreamy waltz step.

"There's many a thorn hidden in these roses. Nothing beautiful is harmless, I suppose," Laura said.

"You're beautiful, and you'd never harm anyone," Maggie retorted.

Laura smiled wryly. "I wouldn't."

Maggie gave her a puzzled look, cocking her head to one side and setting her dark curls bobbing. Her cheeks were rosy with happiness. "Don't be deep and thoughtful today, Laura. I have so much to tell you."

"I'm sure you do," Laura said with resignation. "Let's go for a walk. Then you can tell me everything and we won't be overheard."

Maggie's eyes glowed, and she kissed Laura's cheek. "I knew you would say so."

Reluctantly, Laura went to the gate and let herself out. Maggie hurried to her side, hooking an arm confidingly around her waist. But before Maggie could open her heart, Jack rounded the corner and waved. The girls stood, waiting in silence for him to approach.

Jack sought Laura's gaze as he joined them. "Where've you been, Laura? I haven't seen you anywhere lately."

"I've only been working," Laura answered. She looked across the rooftops, following the path of a cloud.

"Slaving at the books, I suppose, now that you're going to college," Jack guessed.

Maggie's mouth dropped open. "Laura, I thought we'd settled that!"

"Don't you think she should go?" Jack asked, his eyebrows disappearing under his tumbled hair.

"Of course not," Maggie said with a toss of her head. "It's the most foolish thing I ever heard."

"I think she should go," Jack broke in stoutly. "She's as smart as a whip, and there's nothing to stop her."

Laura shook her head. "I'm not going."

Maggie squeezed her arm. "Good, I'm glad you got over that silly idea."

Laura met Jack's eyes, and the care and regret she saw in them threatened to make her cry. His sympathy was more than she could bear. She looked away, close to panic.

"Go away, Jack," she said, more roughly than she meant. "I don't want to talk to you right now."

"That's right," Maggie agreed. "We have important matters to discuss."

With a baffled look, Jack dug his hands in his pockets and slouched away, kicking at pebbles. Laura watched him go, wishing from the bottom of her heart that she felt differently about him. But she could not bring herself to love him.

And she could not indulge herself in his compassion either. She needed to keep from breaking apart, and his kindness would only hasten her collapse. And to take his love and sympathy just to soothe her own bruised heart would be dishonest. Laura wished she could explain it to him, to tell him how much she valued his loyalty. But she couldn't.

"Now," Maggie said in a confidential tone as they turned their steps down the street. She tucked her arm through Laura's. "I have the most wonderful, magical news to tell you."

"Grant loves you."

"Yes!" Maggie's eyes shone with happiness. "And I'm so in love with him. It almost seems like a holy thing, Laura, honestly it does."

"You're very lucky."

"I know, I feel like the luckiest girl in the world," Maggie breathed. "To tell you the truth, I thought at first that you liked him yourself, but you never spoke of him except to talk about the brainy conversations you had, so I knew you weren't smitten, like I was." Maggie stopped in the street, her face radiant. "I love him so much, I do, I truly do."

Wincing, Laura fussed with the watch pinned to her blouse. Then she saw that her fingers trembled, and she quickly put her hands behind her back to hide their telltale shaking.

"I'm glad," Laura said in a muffled voice.

"And Laura, you must promise to like him for my sake."

Laura stared at Maggie, speechless. Her friend was looking at her so hopefully, so pleadingly, so joyfully, that Laura could hardly believe she was not in a terrible dream. What Maggie was feeling was what Laura had felt. She knew only too well how happy her friend was.

"Do promise you'll like him," Maggie begged again.

"Of course I'll like him for your sake," Laura said in a low voice.

"You're wonderful. Grant admires you so much," Maggie went on blissfully. "I'm sure he only bothered to notice me at first because I'm your friend."

"I'm sure that isn't so." Laura's heart tightened like a clenched fist. She wanted to scream, or cry, or fall in a heap on the sidewalk.

"Well, he does esteem you, and I know he enjoys your company," Maggie said with a laugh. "I hope you'll go about with us often."

"No, I couldn't intrude," Laura whispered, turning to stare hard at a red-patterned dress in a shop window.

Maggie peered at her from the side. "Why, Laura MacKenzie, you're crying!"

Quickly, Laura wiped a tear from her eye and

caught her friend in an embrace. "It's only because I'm so happy for you, that's all."

"Oh, Laura, you're the best friend in the world!"

They stood with their arms around one another, both crying for love—Maggie, who had fallen in and out of love so often, and Laura, who had never done so before, and who feared she never would again.

"Oh, can you believe us?" Maggie said, breaking away with a teary laugh. She took Laura's hand, and they strolled toward the harbor. "I hardly imagined when I went to the Resplendent that I would never have to work there at all!"

"No, you won't have to work there, now," Laura agreed. They stood looking out across the water. They could see the grand hotel from their vantage point, proud as a castle, spread out along the crown of the Neck.

"Perhaps you could take my job," Maggie began. "Or you could find another one there as soon as possible. After all, you might meet someone as wonderful as Grant too."

Laura found that she had to look away from the sight of the hotel. Her eyes rested on a handbill tacked to the wall of a nearby building, which proclaimed that the great Sarah Bernhardt would be appearing at the grand opening of the Resplendent. Laura stared at it.

"Maybe I should work there," she said, more to herself than to Maggie. "If I have to stay in Marblehead, it might as well be at the Resplendent."

"Oh, yes, Laura, I agree," Maggie said eagerly. "You're sure to meet someone if you do."

And see great actresses, and hear an echo of news and art, Laura added to herself. Perhaps there, at least, she might be a spectator of the world, if she couldn't be in it.

Chapter Ten

WHEN LAURA RETURNED to the Wild Rose a little later she slipped inside quietly, not wanting to be seen, and hurried to her room. Carefully, she opened the secret windowsill cache once more and knelt before it. What at first had seemed like hopeful signs, now looked very different. The doll, the cross, and the grass bracelet seemed like the remnants of ship-wrecked lives, secreted away against hostile elements.

Laura looked at them for several moments, not touching them. The hearts that had loved these treasures must have ached as hers did now. She rested her forehead on the sill, closing her eyes, too heartsick to think or pray or cry, just wishing with a mute helplessness for the hands that had hidden those treasures to soothe her.

But it was not to be, could never be. She stood up, and opening the drawer of her desk, withdrew her diary. Laura placed it among the objects buried in the wall, wedging it between the laths, and then hid it all again with the board.

Drawing a deep breath, she turned her back on her hidden diary, and left her room. Downstairs, she met her mother in the hallway.

"Will you take this into the parlor, dear?" Mrs. Mac-Kenzie said, handing over a tray laden with tea service and muffins.

"Yes," Laura replied automatically. She turned, but then paused and looked back. "Who's here, Mother?"

Mrs. MacKenzie held Laura's gaze for a long moment. "It's Miss Shaw," she said quietly.

Laura sighed. "Don't worry, and don't let Father get in a fuss either. I'll tell her again that I'm not interested in college."

"She's here with a guest," Mrs. MacKenzie said. "She didn't come to argue with us about college, she hasn't mentioned a word of it."

"Oh." Laura frowned down at the tea tray, feeling deflated. "Oh, I see."

"Now, go along," Mrs. MacKenzie said, steering Laura toward the parlor and giving her a gentle shove.

With some reluctance, Laura walked down the corridor and shifted the tray onto her hip so that she could open the parlor door.

Miss Shaw and her companion broke off in the middle of their conversation and looked around as Laura entered.

"Good afternoon, Miss Shaw," Laura murmured, looking down at the tray.

She carried the tea service in and arranged the cups and pot on a small cherry table. From the corner of her eye, she took in Miss Shaw's companion, an elegant, well-dressed woman whose gray hair framed a lovely face. Her hands were heavy with rings.

"Laura, I'd like to introduce a very old friend of mine," Miss Shaw said.

"Not so very old, I hope," the woman pleaded. She let out a silvery laugh and turned to Laura with her hand extended. There was a faint scent of lavender as she moved. "Mrs. Cavendish. I'm pleased to meet you, Miss MacKenzie."

"How do you do?" Laura replied, shaking her hand. She held the tray at her side, unwilling to go, unwilling to stay.

Miss Shaw began to pour tea into the cups. "Mrs. Cavendish is here from Boston for the day. We were at Wellesley together, Eveline and I."

Laura pressed her lips together. "Miss Shaw, I hope I don't sound rude, or ungrateful, but if you've brought your friend here in order to—to—" She broke off, knowing how shamefully ungracious she sounded.

Mrs. Cavendish picked out a lump of sugar with the tongs and dropped it into her cup. She eyed Laura quizzically.

"She suspects me of nefarious scheming," Miss Shaw said to Mrs. Cavendish.

Mrs. Cavendish stirred her·tea. "So it seems."

Blushing, Laura began to back toward the door. "I

130

beg your pardon," she said. "I'm afraid I've been terribly conceited and rude."

"Oh, Laura," Miss Shaw burst out irritably. "Don't be ridiculous."

Laura stopped at the door, utterly at a loss. She looked from one woman to the other and shrugged helplessly. "I'm sorry. I don't know what you want. Not that you should want anything, but . . ."

Mrs. Cavendish smiled and patted the settee beside her. "Stay and visit for a few minutes, Miss MacKenzie. I've heard so much about you, and I'm so interested in your house. It's a wonderful old building."

"Yes," Laura agreed with a slight hesitation. She lowered herself onto the settee. "The tavern—that's the part at the side and front—that part of the house dates from the 1680's."

"And this wing that we're in, I judge to have been built in the mid-eighteenth century?" Mrs. Cavendish asked. She sipped her tea and looked appraisingly around the room.

"My ancestor Matthew MacKenzie built it with his father John, and then his son Lieutenant John MacKenzie—"

"Of the Marblehead Militia?" Miss Shaw put in.

"That's right," Laura agreed, warming to her tale. "One-armed John, they called him after the War of Independence."

"I've read of the exploits of the Marblehead sailors in the Revolution," Mrs. Cavendish said. She lowered her voice. "They say those men were either drunk or fighting the English or both."

Laura grinned and met Miss Shaw's eyes. "Well, they do say that. Fortunately, One-armed John left off both when he came back here to marry and add on to the inn."

"The architecture of these old houses is fascinating to me," Mrs. Cavendish said with an admiring look around the room. "We have a dear friend who is an architect, Mr. Sullivan—"

"Mr. Louis Sullivan?" Laura asked, her eyes wide.

The woman beamed. "Yes, that's right, dear Louis."

Miss Shaw let out an unladylike snort of laughter. " 'Dear Louis,' " she mimicked. Turning to Laura, she said, "Mrs. Cavendish opens her doors to everyone, and everyone comes. Mary Cassatt, Clarence Darrow, H. G. Wells . . ."

As Miss Shaw reeled off the list of artists, writers, and statesmen, Laura turned wondering eyes on Mrs. Cavendish. The woman was blushing with gratification.

"They only know I'm always happy to see them and they eat well at my table," she said modestly.

"They come because you're their queen bee," Miss Shaw retorted. "They bring you their puzzles and you sort them out."

Laura marveled again at the beautiful, talented, and accomplished Mrs. Cavendish, yet a nagging question formed itself in her head.

"Doesn't—does your husband mind that you spend

so much time with intellectuals?" she asked, knowing how uncouth it sounded.

Miss Shaw sniffed, and stirred her tea. "Hardly."

"Mr. Cavendish is as generous as can be," Mrs. Cavendish said.

Laura glanced at Miss Shaw, wondering if perhaps the marriage was a distant one. But the moment the thought entered her head, her old teacher looked at her sharply.

"He dotes on her," Miss Shaw said, almost reading Laura's thoughts. "He thinks she's the most marvellous person in the world and her children adore her."

"Oh, Julia," Mrs. Cavendish murmured, coloring. "Don't continue."

"It was the love match of the century," Miss Shaw continued as though her friend hadn't spoken. "When Arthur Cavendish courted her, it was the romantic sensation of Boston."

To Laura's surprise, there was a glow in Mrs. Cavendish's face, exactly as there had been in Maggie's. Even at her age, Mrs. Cavendish was obviously in love, and well loved in return.

"You're very lucky," Laura said for the second time that day.

"Miss MacKenzie," Mrs. Cavendish said, putting one hand on Laura's. "I hope you will come to one of my evenings sometime when you can get to Boston."

Flattered and flustered, Laura reached for the tea tray and rose from her seat. "That's very kind of you, but

I couldn't possibly mix with your company. I would be hopelessly out of place."

"Laura."

Miss Shaw fixed her with a stern eye and stared at her so severely that Laura began to blush. "Laura, stand up," her teacher scolded.

"I—I am standing, Miss Shaw," Laura stammered.

Her teacher looked at Mrs. Cavendish and spoke with sharp sarcasm. "It shouldn't surprise you that when I finally choose a protégée, she turns out to be the most stubborn girl in Marblehead."

"Judging by what I've heard you say about her father, I assumed she'd be on the obstinate side," Mrs. Cavendish said.

Laura was growing more confused and chagrined by the moment. Her teacher was obviously cross and impatient with her, but she didn't know why. She backed uncomfortably to the door, wishing the interview would end as quickly as possible.

"Miss MacKenzie," Mrs. Cavendish said, coming to her rescue. "Please call on me anytime you come to Boston."

"Thank you," Laura murmured. She met Miss Shaw's eyes one more time, and then slipped out of the room.

In the corridor, Laura paused to collect herself. Her thoughts were scattered in a hundred directions. An unreasonable anger at Miss Shaw came flooding over her as she heard the faint murmur of the older women's voices. How unfair, how cruel, to bring to Laura an example of education, wealth, and refinement that Laura was in no position to aspire to. If there was bad blood between Miss Shaw and Laura's father, it was hard and unwarranted for Miss Shaw to hurt him through his daughter.

Scowling fiercely, Laura strode to the kitchen and set the tea tray down with a clatter. Mrs. MacKenzie, peeling potatoes, waited for Laura to speak.

Laura tried to steady her breathing, but found herself dangerously close to tears. She jerked out a chair and sat across from her mother, picking up a small piece of raw potato to nibble on.

"Why does she take such a particular interest in me?" she said petulantly. "She pushes with one hand and yanks back with the other."

Mrs. MacKenzie turned a potato over in her hands, examining it for black spots. "Perhaps you remind her of herself."

"I hope I'm not as starchy as that."

Mrs. MacKenzie smiled faintly, but neither agreed nor disagreed.

Frowning, Laura rubbed the powdery starch from her fingers. "How well did you know her?"

"Not very well," Mrs. MacKenzie said with a distant look in her eyes. "But I knew she was a very fine girl. Not beautiful, but she had a quality to her . . ."

Laura nodded, thinking of the force of Miss Shaw's personality. Abrasive, strict, ambitious, loyal—uncompromising.

"Your father was in love with her, you know."

Laura's head jerked up. She stared at her mother. "He was?"

Mrs. MacKenzie's strong fingers worked around another potato, the knife glinting in the light. "Oh yes, they were regular sweethearts. Every Sunday come rain or shine he went to Salem to court her, and she even moved in here for a while to nurse him through the rheumatic fever. He asked her to marry him, but in the end she wouldn't take him."

"I can't believe it," Laura whispered. She blushed suddenly, looking at her mother's downcast eyes. "How did you—that is . . ."

"Your father insisted that Julia make a choice between him and her ambitions," Mrs. MacKenzie explained. "She wanted an education and told him he wouldn't stand in her way if he loved her, and that was that. They both have tempers, you know."

"I know," Laura said, her mind spinning.

Her mother shrugged. "And so he married me. I was willing to give him what he wanted," she said softly. "I don't regret my choice, and I'm sure Julia does not regret hers."

"Does he contradict her wishes then purely from anger and in spite of my own?" Laura asked in disbelief. "With no consideration for me?"

Her mother shook her head, as though trying to resolve the question in her own mind. "I think you must ask him, if you really want to know."

Laura twined her fingers together in her lap, trying to sort out the tumult inside her head. Her mother quietly continued her work, glancing up from time to time at Laura's pensive face. Distantly, from outside as well as inside the corridors of the house, the sounds of men coming into the tavern for the evening reached the kitchen. She heard Miss Shaw greet Mr. Carter on the street, and knew that the two women had left.

Abruptly, Laura pushed her chair back, reached a lamp down from the mantel and lit the wick.

"It's hardly gone dark yet," her mother observed.

"It seems dark enough to me," Laura said shortly.

She walked out into the corridor. The light from her lamp flowed around her as she walked, and objects and pictures started up out of the dimness, only to fade into the shadows again when she passed. As Laura walked in her circle of light, she found herself more and more upset, more bitter toward her father.

"He has no right to treat me so," she whispered.

When she entered the tavern, Laura sought out her father. He was laughing with Mr. Ledue as he poured beer and skimmed off the foam, and his face was relaxed and happy. Laura felt a stony hardness settle on her. He was thwarting her to spite Miss Shaw. It was the worst injustice he could do to his own daughter.

Laura crossed to the bar, put down the lamp, and stood staring at him until he took notice of her.

"Why, Laura, what is it?" he asked. "You look pale as a ghost."

Laura stared at him for a moment longer and slowly shook her head. "I have forgiven you for hardness and

137

backwardness before this, but you stand in my way through selfishness now, and I can't forgive you."

"What?" Mr. MacKenzie looked quickly around, to see if anyone else had heard her. His patrons were all talking and laughing amongst themselves, however, and did not heed Laura.

"What talk is this?" he asked with blustering indignation, hurrying around from behind the bar.

"Hi, Lem," called out Mr. Braxton. "Have you any sherry wine?"

Laura turned to leave.

"Laura—" her father said.

"Lem?"

"In a moment," Mr. MacKenzie said impatiently, grabbing the lamp and following Laura across the tavern.

Laura knew he was following her. She had nothing to say to him, and did not want to confront him since she couldn't bear to listen to him deny the truth. If she had to listen to him do so, she felt she would scream. She left the tavern, the heels of her shoes ringing loudly on the wooden floors.

"Laura, stop, what do you mean by it?" her father called.

She ducked her head, still refusing to give way to the anger that seemed to burn her like a brand. Her own shadow jumped and swayed ahead of her as her father strode behind her with the lamp.

"Laura, go into the parlor. You owe me an explanation."

Without answering, she turned and went down the

next corridor and into the parlor, where her hard foot-steps were deadened by the worn Turkey carpet. In the room lingered a faint scent of lavender. Laura looked at the chair where she had last seen Miss Shaw, straight-backed, the garnet glowing at her throat.

"Now, perhaps you'll be good enough to tell why you throw hateful accusations at me in my own home," her father said, shutting the door firmly behind him.

Laura turned and faced him. "I hope I don't come to hate you, Father," she said, her anger flaring up in-stantly. "You said Miss Shaw was jealous of me—but it's you who are jealous of her. Jealous that she thrives with-out you, that she made her choice and it wasn't you and now I must suffer for your loss. *I* must!"

"Laura, you don't know what you're talking about," Mr. MacKenzie said, his brows drawing together in a sharp line. His breathing was harsh. "Whatever Miss Shaw told you is a lie."

"It was Mother who told me," Laura flung at him. Her eyes were hot with tears. "I think you're a coward. You didn't trust Miss Shaw to love you after she went to college, and you know you're a fool for it."

"How dare you speak to me that way?" her father shouted.

The lamp trembled in his hand, and Laura could see he was trembling with rage, but she didn't care. At least he would know how much he had hurt her.

"How does a child of mine dare speak to me that way?" he repeated in a choked voice.

"You mean how dare a *daughter* speak that way," Laura said. "Do I remind you of her so much that you would trample all my chances? You would scorn my suggestions for this house and so much as tell me I'm good for nothing but service?"

Laura turned her back on him, not wanting him to see the tears that scalded her eyes. She put her hands to her temples and pressed as hard as she could.

Behind her, Mr. MacKenzie let out a short, sharp gasp, a sound so odd that Laura turned. His face in the lamplight was pale and shining with sweat, and his lips seemed almost blue. He stared at her, shaking his head.

"Father?" Laura stood where she was, still too shaken with emotion to move.

He brought one hand to his throat and set the lamp down as he fought for breath. His shaking hand went to his chest. "Laura," he gasped, leaning against the sideboard. "Get your mother."

Suddenly, he moved his arm in a convulsive gesture, as though grabbing for something, and swept everything off the sideboard. The lamp tipped over as he fell.

"Father!"

The glass lamp crashed on the wooden floor, and burning oil flowed quickly to the edge of the carpet. Laura stamped at the flames, but the sight of her father on his hands and knees made her sick with alarm. She ran to him, and knelt at his side. He was breathing raggedly, his eyes squeezed shut, and Laura could see the

140

sweat pouring from his face as the room darted into sudden brilliance.

She lunged upward, reaching for the door, and as she wrenched it open she screamed "FIRE!" as loud as she could.

Chapter Eleven

 "FATHER, STAND UP, let me help you," Laura said urgently.

"No—put out the fire," he choked. "The house—"

The wallpaper was crackling and whispering as the fire curled its edges. Laura's heart raced with fear. She looked around frantically. The fire seemed to flow like water, lapping across the old carpet and licking the bottoms of the drapes with shocking speed. Smoke rolled around the room. Desperate, Laura tried to help her father stand, but he could not raise himself and he was too big for her strength.

Laura ran to the door and screamed again, beating at a spark that landed on her dress. The far corners of the parlor sprang into light. "God, somebody help us!" she screamed again, knowing that the old mazelike inn muffled sound through its twisting passages.

On the floor among scattered scrimshaw and pewter mugs lay an old conch-shell horn. Laura grabbed it and drew a deep breath, almost choking on smoke. She blew one long bass note, the tone reverberating through the halls and echoing deeply in the bones of the house.

Smoke wreathed around her, and Laura ran back to the windows, yanking at a set of curtains and using them to beat at the rioting flames. Half the floor was on fire near her father. Laura sobbed and ran to him.

"Can't you stand? Father! Stand up!"

Footsteps thundered down the hallway, and shouts for assistance echoed through the building. The fire filled the room with sound, like the ocean roaring in a cove. Laura screamed as a burning drape cascaded to the floor with a billowing wave of sparks and smoke and heat.

"Laura!" Men surged into the room, beating at the fire with their hands and coats. Laura was coughing and choking, tears running down her soot-stained face.

"My father!" she yelled, pointing to where he lay.

Someone grabbed Laura around the legs with a coat, and she looked down as she fell, noticing in surprise that her hem was on fire. She was rolled across the floor and then set upright and shoved roughly from the room.

The corridor was a mad, dark chaos. Men with buckets jostled vainly against one another in the narrow passage, shouting as they passed water, spilling more on the floor than made it into the blazing room. One man slipped, plunging into another man in the choking, smoky dimness. Off in the street, fire bells clanged wildly.

"It's no use!" one man shouted. "The house is dry as a tinderbox!"

There was a roaring crash and splintering of glass as a window broke out, and flame and smoke surged out into the hallway. "Look out!" someone yelled in panic.

Laura cowered against the wall, the pain in her legs throbbing with each terrified beat of her heart. "Where's my father?" she screamed as Mr. Trelawney ran by. "Get my father out!"

Someone grabbed her hand and dragged her away, almost jerking her off her feet. The smell of burning wood and paint rasped at her lungs as Laura struggled for air and slid on the wet wood floors. Crying and coughing, she burst out into the street.

"Laura! Laura, where are you?" Mrs. MacKenzie screamed. "Where's Lem?"

The pump wagons filled Front Street, the horses tossing their heads as men shouted commands and bells clanged. Children screamed when the water wagons shifted and backed into the crowd, and one frightened horse lashed out with its hooves before a woman wrapped a shawl around its head. The fire volunteers dragged a hose into the Wild Rose, ordering people out. A dog ran frantically among the horses, barking wildly. Flames reached upward into the sunset sky, red and gold and black.

"Mother!"

"Laura, where are you? LAURA!"

Laura staggered through the crowd and fell sobbing against her mother and brothers, who stood helplessly by. Another roaring crash sent a blazing shower of sparks up into the sky as the roof of the east wing fell in. All around them, the street was filled with awestruck neighbors, neighing horses, shouting firemen. It was like a scene from hell.

"It's a rabbit warren of passages!" the fire captain shouted to a group of pumpers. "Aim the water there and there," he ordered, pointing. "Before the fire spreads on the west side of the house!"

"Laura!" Maggie's voice cut through the clamor. She ran to Laura and hugged her tight.

"My father," Laura sobbed. "The oil lamp—it spread so fast!" Laura's sobs came from deep down, wrenching through her chest as though each one was being torn from her heart. Her lungs were raw with smoke. "Mother—I tried to stop it."

"Where is he?" Mrs. MacKenzie demanded, clutching Laura's arms. The boys, David and Henry, cried into Mrs. MacKenzie's apron, too frightened to watch the scene of destruction.

"Mrs. MacKenzie, your husband is over here," a soot-blackened fireman said. Mrs. MacKenzie hurried after him.

On the edge of the crowd Miss Shaw stood motionless, tears streaking her cheeks. With a groan, Laura covered her face with her hands and sank to her knees as her entire life went up in flames.

Laura awoke early the next morning, staring at an unfamiliar ceiling. She turned her eyes to the left and saw white muslin curtains gently moving at the window, the faint pale sky of dawn beyond and the home-smell of salt air coming through them. By the window was a ladderback chair, a marble-top washstand, a studded sea chest.

Sighing, Laura looked to her right and saw her brothers sleeping beside her in the wide bed. She did not know why they were in the bed. The muffled, dreamlike aura of sleep still clouded her mind, but gradually, she became aware of the stinging of her legs and the acrid smell of the clothes lying on the floor.

"Oh, God," she whispered, closing her eyes again. Tears slipped from between her lashes and ran back into her hair, wetting the pillow. Against her eyelids, the light of morning was as red as fire.

Not wanting to wake her brothers, Laura climbed out of the bed. Her legs were bandaged, but the burns were not very large nor very deep. At the foot of the bed lay one of Maggie's dresses. Laura put it on, her fingers trembling so much that she could hardly fasten the buttons. She cast a frightened look at Henry as he rolled over, his forehead creased.

Then she tiptoed from the room, out into the upstairs hallway of the Ship. Laura closed the door behind her. The Handys had won the argument at last, it seemed, and now the MacKenzies must take hospitality from their age-old rivals. Laura shook her head at the bitterness and irony of it, since she knew how hard it would be for her parents to bear.

From nearby, muffled voices reached her. Another door opened, and Dr. Merrivale stepped out into the passage, snapping his leather bag shut.

"Laura, how do your legs feel?" he asked when he saw her.

"Not too bad—my father?" Laura looked at the door behind him.

"Resting well," the doctor said. "He had a heart attack. Mild, however. He should make a fine recovery."

Laura gripped her hands together to keep them from shaking. "Thank you," she whispered, her eyes still on the closed door.

Dr. Merrivale scratched at his ginger side-whiskers and smiled, cocking his head toward the door. "He is awake, and I know would like to see his daughter."

"Oh, but it's so much my fault," Laura whispered. Hot tears welled up in her eyes and spilled over, and she brushed them miserably away.

"I don't know about that," Dr. Merrivale said. He opened the door before she could stop him and looked inside. "Lem, your daughter's here to see you."

Laura drew a shaky breath and walked forward as the doctor ushered her in. In a large, four-poster bed her father lay propped up on pillows. Mrs. MacKenzie sat in a chair by the bedside, holding a cup of coffee. They both looked at Laura as she walked slowly into the room, and the doctor shut the door on them with quiet tact. Lemuel MacKenzie's face was pale and weary, and there were circles under his eyes.

"Father, I'm so sorry," Laura said at last. "I'm sorry for what I said, and for upsetting you so."

He cleared his throat. "No, don't say it, Laura. The doctor's made it clear enough it was my own stubborn fault."

"But if I'd been less trouble to you, this wouldn't have happened," Laura said.

Mrs. MacKenzie let out an audible sigh, rose from her chair and went to the window. Laura saw her shaking her head. Heartsick, Laura looked back at her father, who was struggling to raise himself higher against the pillows. Laura went to him and helped him sit straighter, all the bitterness she'd felt toward him gone far away.

He took her hands in his and pulled her down to sit beside him on the bed. With her hands in his, she couldn't wipe away the tears that kept spilling on her cheeks. She looked down.

"Laura, you said many a true thing last night, and have been saying true things for months," her father said quietly. "I've always been a stubborn man and don't like to listen when I know I'm in the wrong, but that doesn't make the truth any less. Who knows, if we'd put in the gas, as you kept asking . . ."

Laura squeezed her eyes shut tight and bowed her head even more. "No," she groaned, hurt with an even deeper pain than she'd felt so far. "Don't say it now! Don't say so now when our home is destroyed."

"Not completely," Mrs. MacKenzie spoke up. "The

oldest part, the old tavern and the rooms above escaped. Your room escaped, Laura."

Mr. MacKenzie clasped Laura's hands between his own. "And we'll start again from there. It's more than what Ian and Flora MacKenzie had when they arrived in this town. We've weathered war and sickness and hurricane, and will weather this. I swear it."

Laura straightened her back. "You'll rebuild the Wild Rose?" she asked.

Mrs. MacKenzie turned away from the window. "We'll have to send the boys to Aunt Lavinia in New Bedford until we can bring the business back. But we have the insurance, so we can build again."

What Laura would do, or where she would go, remained unasked. She hugged her elbows to her sides and shivered.

"I want to see the house," she said, willing herself not to cry. She stood up awkwardly and looked from her mother to father. "I want to know what's left. Can I go?"

Her parents exchanged a sad glance.

"It's as you like, Laura," Mr. MacKenzie said. "I've done with telling you what you can and can't do."

Laura bowed her head in weary acknowledgment and left the room. She walked stiffly from the Ship and down the street, praying that no one spoke to her or offered their condolence. Her shins smarted beneath the bandages, but it was nothing compared to the pain she felt when she turned the corner and beheld the wreckage of the Wild Rose Inn—the wreckage of her home.

Charred and smoldering wet timbers lay in a heap

on the site, two brick chimneys pointing up at the sky. Beside the smoking rubble, the old tavern sat alone and pitifully small. Two children from across the street stood among the burned remains, but when they saw her they ran off.

Shaking her head, Laura opened the gate, where the roses burned with their own unvanquished fire. She stroked the petals of one bloom, and they fluttered through her fingers and onto her feet. The red petals blew among ashes and blackened splinters of wood, drifting against the doorstep of the old house.

Laura opened the door. The tavern smelled of smoke, and her footsteps rang hollowly in the empty room. She walked through it slowly, running her fingers across the tops of the tables and the backs of chairs. There should have been men sitting by the fireplace, arguing over their beer. There should have been the scent of bread, and of fish stew, not the acrid tang of burning.

Laura stood there, her eyes closed, as though by the force of will she could make the old seamen appear. But the room was silent around her. With an effort, she steeled herself to open the door that had led to the rest of the house. It stuck in its frame, swollen with water. Laura put her shoulder to it, shoving hard. The door opened with a squeak, and she stood staring into space.

The burned remains of a bench lay across her path in what only yesterday had been a hallway. Laura stepped around it, her mind flooded with images of what should have surrounded her: the chestnut paneling, the photographs and maps, the doors—her home. Above her, where the ceiling had once creaked with footsteps, the sky was blue, and a gull winged out to the sea on the breeze. The kitchen hearth, bricks black with soot, yawned like an empty mouth, and the old coal stove, bent and buckled from the blaze, sat among the ruins.

Laura bent down to retrieve the scorched remains of a metal pot. She drew her breath in sharply and dropped it: the metal was still warm. The pot fell with a dull clang among the grit and ashes.

Too late. Too late. The refrain ran dully through her mind. There was no business now to urge toward progress and the future. There were no lamps to fit for gas, no sinks to run plumbing for. The MacKenzies had paid a dear price for balking at progress, and the future would run roughshod over anyone else who stubbornly, foolishly remained behind.

A murmur of voices reached Laura's ears, almost as though the voices of her ancestors were whispering through the ashes. She turned her head, and saw Jack and Grant framed by a burnt-out hole facing Front Street. They stopped, and looked at her questioningly.

Laura's heart turned inside her to see Grant and the expression of sympathy on his lean face. He made as though to move toward her, but Jack put a hand on his arm and said something too low for Laura to catch. Grant nodded, and turned away as Jack came on.

Without speaking, Jack took hold of Laura's hand. They stood together in silence, their heads bowed.

"Jack . . ." Laura's voice broke.

"I'm so sorry," he said. He turned to look at her, the morning sun making him squint. "I'd do anything to help you, you know that."

"I know," she said. She let her gaze travel to the garden, which was trampled and littered with burned timbers.

"What'll you do?"

Laura sighed. "Go into service, what else can I do?" she said as though to herself. "I have no job here, obviously. I tried to stop the fire, but it got away from me."

Jack shook his head, frowning. "Laura, you saved your father's life—that's worth more than a house."

"But what are we but our house?" she asked. "Two hundred years we've been here, and not been anything but the Wild Rose."

"Oh, Laura, you're so wrong."

She gripped his hand tightly, giving him a sad smile. He wanted to help her so much, the yearning in his eyes spoke so loudly and plainly of his wish to make things right for her that her heart went out to him. "I'll be fine, Jack," she said hoarsely. "Don't worry about me."

Jack twined his fingers through hers, his face flushed and earnest and filled with hope. "Marry me, Laura. Marry me now," he pleaded. "You can sit in the parlor all day reading books, if that's what you want."

A tear fell onto their hands as Laura ducked her head. Her heart ached, for him as much as for herself and her own ruined dreams. "I can't," she whispered.

"Yes, you can," he said urgently. "I know you don't

love me, but you might come to, and I would do anything to make you happy."

"I know." She wiped her cheek against her shoulder. The blue cotton against her skin felt strange, and she remembered with a start that it was Maggie's dress she was wearing. A forlorn, helpless sadness swept through her, that it was not Grant who held her hand so tightly or stood beside her on the site of her ruined house. Jack had always been true to her, but it was not enough.

"Laura?" Jack's voice was full of sadness too.

She looked down at their clasped hands and gently untwined her fingers from his. She stroked his hand, and then let go. "I can't, Jack. I'm sorry, but I can't."

"Is it because of Grant?" he asked in a bitter voice.

Laura flinched. "Please understand . . . I don't know what I am, or who I am," she said. "There seems to be no place for me. I don't fit. I don't know how to be who people want me to be."

He reached down to pick up a blown rose petal, and smoothed it between his fingers. "It's not because you read books and have ideas and love to know things that Grant doesn't love you, Laura."

"Yes, it is."

"No, he doesn't love you because he doesn't," Jack insisted. "If you'd flirted and acted the silly helpless female, he still wouldn't have loved you the way you want him to. Don't deceive yourself. It has nothing to do with wanting to go to college or having ambitions."

Jack's words stung. Laura ran into the trampled garden, desperate to get away from the truth of what he said.

"He just didn't love you," Jack called. "It's nobody's fault, least of all yours."

Laura didn't want to cry, but she couldn't help it. The tears fell and she stopped in her tracks, hanging her head in misery. An iron candlestick, misshapen and covered with ashes, rolled away from her foot. She stared at it, thinking of the light that Grant had lit for her, thinking of all the lights she had fought so hard to bring into her life.

Now the sun poured in around the smoking timbers of the house, flooding every desolate detail with harsh, glaring brilliance. Laura closed her eyes and cried.

Chapter Twelve

JACK WALKED AWAY. Laura heard him leave, and for a moment, felt a tearing impulse to run after him. But she stayed where she was among the ruins and the smell of smoke.

Then, as though to keep herself from calling out to him, Laura ran out of the garden. She wouldn't let herself think of what she had turned down, or what she would have to face now. She ran on and found that she was headed for the old burying ground. At the bottom of the hill she stopped.

There, in the dappled shade beneath the elm tree where she stood, she had begun to fall in love with Grant. There she had felt as though the world had just been revealed to her, as though the sun had come from behind clouds and bathed everything in gold. It had been fool's gold. Grant had opened her eyes to something and made her yearn for more, but now it was beyond her grasp.

Clenching her fists, she began to climb the path, up among the gravestones. The breeze blew against her hot face but she trudged on steadily over the granite outcroppings and through the tall, nodding grasses that waved as she passed, until she reached the top.

Laura turned and looked out across Marblehead, across the harbor to the glittering ocean beyond. Sailboats beat across the water, heeling in the wind, and below her, smoke rose from the chimneys of the town and was whisked away on the breeze. She could see the Resplendent from where she stood among the oldest graves of Marblehead.

With a frown, she collected her skirts beneath her and sat down on the grass, resting her chin on her knees. Around her, the quiet burying ground spread out like a map of her own history, her family name calling from every side.

For several minutes, she brooded over the markers that bore the words of long-dead poets and divines, and that proclaimed battles won and lost—against the ocean, against foreign foes, against hardship. MacKenzies had perished at sea, had given their lives for independence and honor and love. When she lifted her gaze again, there was the far-off hotel like a messenger from the next century. The hotel stood against the horizon, its windows flashing and telegraphing what it was willing to offer to a girl: a promise of work, the vague, tenuous hope of meeting some man.

"I won't."

The sound of her own voice startled her. A robin

flitted across the path of her vision in a series of swooping arcs, and then settled in the grass. Laura stood up, her skirts whipping around her legs. "I won't settle for that. I don't have to settle for that."

She stood at the crest of the hill over the town, shaking her head in defiance. Then, hardly knowing what she did, Laura plunged down the hill, filled with strange rebellion. The grass was smooth under her feet and the gravestones blurred as she ran past. At the bottom of the hill she turned down a crooked street. A coal wagon stood outside a house, and she dodged around it, ducking into an alley where a dog barked at her from behind a fence. Breathless, she turned a corner and came out in front of Miss Shaw's house. She banged on the door with both fists.

"Miss Shaw!"

She knocked again, near panic. The door swung open suddenly, and there was her teacher with an expression of surprise on her face.

"Laura?"

"Help me!" Laura gasped. "Help me get to college, I'll do anything! I'll take a job there, work for my tuition and board—please!"

Miss Shaw drew her brows together. Her cat twined around her legs. "Is this what you want? What you really want?"

"Yes," Laura said, panting and nodding. "Yes, it is, it truly is. I want to be something, make something of myself, not wait for someone to do it for me."

A smile of great beauty transformed her teacher's

157

face. Miss Shaw hugged Laura tight, her fingers hard against Laura's shoulders. "Come in. I have a surprise for you."

Trembling, and almost frightened by what she had done, Laura followed Miss Shaw into the green hallway. The house smelled of roasting chicken, of lavender, and of beeswax.

Miss Shaw turned suddenly, her face in shadow. "How is your father?"

Laura tried to read her teacher's expression, tried to interpret her tone of voice, but couldn't. "Dr. Merrivale says he will be fine, and my parents will rebuild the house," she said.

For a moment, Miss Shaw did not speak. Then she drew her breath in slowly. "I am very glad to hear that," she said in a low voice. "Very glad."

"Miss Shaw?" Laura began hesitantly.

"Yes?"

Laughter rang out suddenly from the library. Laura left her question unasked. "You have company," she murmured.

Her teacher put her hand on the doorknob. "Mrs. Cavendish is here again, like Providence itself. Come in, she particularly came to see you."

Laura's heart tripped. She followed Miss Shaw into the library, and halted on the threshold. On one side of Mrs. Cavendish sat a girl Laura's age, and on the other sat a young man a few years older, who stood politely when Laura entered.

"Miss MacKenzie, I was so sorry to hear about the fire," Mrs. Cavendish said, rising and coming forward with her hands outstretched.

"Oh, thank you," Laura said.

Mrs. Cavendish took Laura by the hand. "May I introduce my children to you, Miss MacKenzie? My daughter Elizabeth, and my son William."

"How do you do?" Laura said automatically.

Elizabeth, a plump young woman with a smiling pixie face, stepped forward, petticoats rustling. "Mother hasn't stopped talking about you, I thought you'd be much taller, somehow!" she exclaimed as she shook Laura's hand. "I expected a giant!"

"Oh, did you?" Laura asked. She blushed, knowing that she'd been complimented, as odd as it was.

William shook Laura's hand too. He had blue eyes and a good-humored expression. "Don't mind anything she says," he said with a fond look at his sister. "Liz never thinks before she speaks."

"Don't mind either of them, Miss MacKenzie," Mrs. Cavendish laughed. "Now come sit down. I have an offer to make you," Mrs. Cavendish said. She put her arm through Laura's and led her to the sofa.

In a daze, Laura sat beside the elegant woman. In her borrowed dress, and with her emotions so scattered, she felt at a complete loss beside the well-dressed, cheerful Cavendish family. Miss Shaw sat in her armchair, and the gray-striped cat leaped up and began kneading her lap.

159

"Don't you want to know what Mrs. Cavendish has to say?" Miss Shaw prompted, not unkindly.

"Yes, I beg your pardon," Laura said.

Mrs. Cavendish took one of Laura's hands in her own. "Now, my dear, I was greatly impressed by you yesterday, and very shocked and disappointed to hear that with all your promise, your family can't afford to send you to college."

Again, Laura's heart began a wild beating. She held her breath, and her hand shook within Mrs. Cavendish's grasp.

"I want you to go to Wellesley College, Miss Mac-Kenzie," Mrs. Cavendish said, pressing her hand to steady it. When Laura looked blank, the woman added, "I wish to sponsor you."

The color flooded to Laura's cheeks and her eyes stung with tears. "No, you—I'm so grateful, but you don't—"

"Say yes, please, Miss MacKenzie," Elizabeth broke in, leaning forward eagerly in her chair. "I'm to go myself, and I'm terrified. We could live together, and study, and it would be wonderful to have an ally."

"She doesn't make the offer lightly," Miss Shaw said. "Will you accept?"

Awestruck, Laura looked from Mrs. Cavendish to Miss Shaw. Her teacher was watching her, urging her, challenging her. The Cavendish family waited.

Laura raised her chin. "Yes."

"Wonderful!" Elizabeth cried, clapping her hands. She grabbed her mother by the arm and drew her from the sofa. "I claim all her attention, now, Mother. She's mine."

Mrs. Cavendish gave up her seat with good grace and William clapped one hand to his forehead. "It sounds as though you think Mother's just bought you a mechanical toy you can't wait to play with."

"She didn't mean that," Laura spoke up, giving Elizabeth a smile. "She's only glad to have company."

"That's true," Elizabeth agreed, settling comfortably beside Laura. "I'm sure you're not at all intimidated at the thought of going to college."

"But I am," Laura said with a breathless laugh. "Scared witless. And I can hardly believe it's really to happen."

Miss Shaw and Mrs. Cavendish crossed the room to the window and began a low conversation. William pulled his chair closer to the sofa.

"I have to tell you, Miss MacKenzie," he began. "Elizabeth is a chatterbox and will bend your ear all night if you aren't careful."

"He only says that because he was furious when I kept the senator all to myself last Friday," Elizabeth said, narrowing her eyes at her brother.

"But I particularly wanted to discuss transportation with him," William complained.

Elizabeth tossed her head, clearly not at all cowed by her brother. "Ha, you did not, you great impostor. We were having a fascinating conversation about a play by George Bernard Shaw that you didn't see, and you were just jealous at being left out."

"What play was it?" Laura asked, hoping it was one she had read.

"*Mrs. Warren's Profession,*" Elizabeth said. "Not his best play, but it raises some good ideas and the senator was very interested in my opinion."

It was clear to see that for all Elizabeth's light manner, her mind was keen. Like Maggie, she was lively and quick tongued, but also perfectly comfortable debating.

"I doubt you're as terrified of college as you make out," Laura said with a grin. "I think it's a pretense you enjoy for the drama."

"I might exaggerate," Elizabeth admitted, examining her fingernails.

"You know her well already," William said to Laura. To his sister he added, "There's no point trying to bamboozle Miss MacKenzie, so don't even try. She's too perceptive for you."

Laura blushed with pleasure. "Are you at college, too, Mr. Cavendish?" she asked shyly.

"Oh, call him William, he'll get so conceited," Elizabeth broke in. "He's at Harvard. He's brilliant, which he already knows so he's already conceited about that."

"Is that right?" Laura arched her brows, her eyes twinkling.

William shrugged. "If she says so, it must be so. Elizabeth knows everything. What am I so brilliant at, Lizzie?"

"Oh, he can do everything and anything," Elizabeth announced with an airy wave of her hand. "You should

162

see him go at the Latin like a demon. And horseshoe throwing? Without parallel. Eating muffins? Equally un-equalled."

Laura could not help laughing. "How many muffins can he eat at a sitting?"

"You're sure to find out," Elizabeth said. "I made him promise to come to Wellesley every Friday to take me to tea."

"She's afraid she won't get enough interesting conversation without me," William teased.

"Maybe I won't need you after all," Elizabeth shot back. "Now that Laura will be with me, I think I can safely tell you to stay in Cambridge."

William grinned and met Laura's eyes. "I believe I should come as planned. Every Friday."

"I'm not sure, but I think I've heard a rumor that there are quite a lot of muffins at Wellesley College," Laura told him in a speculative tone. "In fact, cakes and biscuits too."

"That settles it, then," he said, clapping his hands on his knees. He looked at his sister. "You're saddled with me, Liz."

Elizabeth frowned, looking from Laura to William and back again. "I believe it's you William intends to eat all that pastry with, Laura. If I'm not mistaken, and I never am, I think he quite admires you."

Blushing wildly, Laura looked down at her hands, and waited for his disclaimer. But he just laughed.

"If you are never mistaken, then you must be right,

Elizabeth. Next to you, Miss MacKenzie is the most admirable girl I've ever met."

Laura raised her eyes to his face, and he smiled at her. Laura smiled back, suddenly craving tea and muffins very much.

"Laura?" came Miss Shaw's voice from the window.

Startled, Laura broke away from William's steady gaze and looked at her teacher. "Yes?"

"Only one thing remains to be settled, my dear," Miss Shaw said. "You'll have to bring your parents around to agreeing. Do you think you can convince them?"

Laura nodded without hesitation and stood up. "I'm sure that I can, Miss Shaw. In fact, I should go now and tell them."

She walked to Mrs. Cavendish and took her hand. "Thank you so much," she said simply. "I'm so grateful."

"You're very welcome," Mrs. Cavendish replied. "I have no doubt that you'll prosper."

Laura turned to Miss Shaw, whose face was silhouetted against the window. "Thank you," Laura said. "Thank you so much."

She turned and smiled widely at Elizabeth, and more shyly at William. "I'll see you very soon, then," she said with a laugh that was half a gasp of surprise. "This is overwhelming."

"Overwhelming?" Elizabeth cried. "Just wait until we sit in on our first lecture."

She shrieked as William clamped a hand over her mouth. He smiled at Laura.

"Looking forward to the muffins, Miss MacKenzie," he said.

"Good-bye."

Jubilant, Laura walked out of the library and made her way down the cool, dim hallway. Then she opened the front door and stepped into a blaze of sunshine.

Follow the sweeping saga of generations
of young MacKenzie women, all growing up
at the Wild Rose Inn.

CLAIRE OF THE WILD ROSE INN
1928

Since her father's death, hardworking Claire MacKenzie has kept afloat the Wild Rose Inn, her family's business for generations. But now that Prohibition has made liquor illegal, the Wild Rose cannot compete with the speakeasies that peddle bootleg alcohol. Claire's brother, Bob, wants to make the Wild Rose a speakeasy, but Claire doesn't want to be involved in any crime—including bootlegging.

Then Claire finds the town drunk shot dead on his boat, and she is drawn into a criminal world. Police Chief Handy inexplicably dismisses the case, but determined, curious Claire wants answers. Her only ally is Hank Logan, a newspaper reporter looking for a scoop. Together they investigate, and every lead brings Claire closer to Hank—and home. It looks as if her brother's efforts to save the inn have gotten him mixed up with gangsters. Claire has learned things are not always what they seem. Whom can she really trust? Will Claire risk her family, the Wild Rose Inn, and her new love for Hank to get to the dangerous truth?

GRACE OF THE WILD ROSE INN
1944

Grace MacKenzie has been achingly lonely since her brother, Mark, and her fiancé, Jimmy Penworthy, have both been sent to the European front. Yet, working hard on the homefront for the war effort, Grace has gained a sense of independence and inner strength.

When the boys finally come home, Grace is heartbroken at how the war has changed her fiancé. A wounded war hero in the eyes of the town, he brags about his experiences while stubbornly insisting that Grace give up her dream to continue to run the Wild Rose Inn after they marry. Grace is confused by her changed feelings for Jimmy—she's angry that he doesn't understand her ambition and yet she feels guilty that she's not the girl Jimmy remembers and still wants her to be.

But Jimmy hasn't returned home alone—his army buddy Mike is everything she'd hoped to find in Jimmy. Where will Grace's heart lead her as she must decide her future, the future of those who love her, and the fate of her family's Wild Rose Inn?

ABOUT THE AUTHOR

Jennifer Armstrong is the author of many books for children and young adults, including the historical novel *Steal Away,* the Pets, Inc. series, and several picture books.

Jennifer Armstrong lives in Saratoga Springs, New York, in a house more than 150 years old that is reputed to have been a tavern. In addition to writing, she raises guide-dog puppies and works in her garden, where roses grow around the garden gate.

THE WILD ROSE INN

A stunning romantic saga of valiant young American women set against a backdrop of 300 years.

By JENNIFER ARMSTRONG

❏ 0-553-29866-6 BRIDIE OF THE WILD ROSE INN, 1695 .....$3.99/$4.99

❏ 0-553-29867-4 ANN OF THE WILD ROSE INN, 1774 ....$3.99/$4.99

❏ 0-553-29909-3 EMILY OF THE WILD ROSE INN, 1858 ......$3.99/$4.99
U.S/Can.
